George Albemarle Bertie Dewar

The South Country Trout Streams

George Albemarle Bertie Dewar

The South Country Trout Streams

ISBN/EAN: 9783744791410

Printed in Europe, USA, Canada, Australia, Japan

Cover: Foto ©Andreas Hilbeck / pixelio.de

More available books at **www.hansebooks.com**

THE SOUTH COUNTRY
TROUT STREAMS

BY

GEORGE A. B. DEWAR

AUTHOR OF "THE BOOK OF THE DRY FLY"

" The trout fisher, like the landscape painter, haunts the loveliest places
of the earth, and haunts them alone."—*Tom Brown at Oxford.*

ILLUSTRATED

LONDON : LAWRENCE AND BULLEN, Ltd.

16 HENRIETTA STREET, COVENT GARDEN

MDCCCXCIX

PREFACE

I TAKE this opportunity of heartily thanking the
many anglers from Kent to Cornwall who have
aided me in my endeavour to obtain trustworthy
information concerning various south country trout
streams; and in particular I must express my
obligations to the Rev. William Awdry, of Ludgershall, Wiltshire, Dr. Comber, Colonel Robert
Waller, Captain Beaumont, Mr. Nash, of Canterbury, the Rev. F. E. Freeman, the Rev. B. T.
Thompson, the Rev. L. I. Procter, His Grace the
Duke of Bedford, the Rev. T. Bentham, the Earl of
Heytesbury, Colonel Mansel, Mr. H. S. Thomas
(author of "The Rod in India"), Colonel Buller,
and Mr. E. Goble, all of whom have been put to
trouble on my behalf. I also desire to acknowledge
the kind assistance of my friend Mr. C. E. Taylor.
Two things have especially struck me in the course
of my inquiries into the condition and the characteristics of our south country trout streams. First,
the large, and, I am afraid, not decreasing, number
of fine waters which are subjected to the most
objectionable forms of pollution, and, secondly, the
lowering of the springs of various chalk streams by
water companies and the like. In not a few
instances I have seen the first of these evils; seen
it and even become fully conscious of it by means

of a sense other than that of the eyes: in others I
have been informed of its existence and mischievous
effects on fish life and fishing by both angling and
non-angling correspondents, who have asked me to
draw attention to the state of their streams.

I am convinced from conversations I have had
with people, who speak with full knowledge and
experience, that the condition of some of our
streams is a menace, not only to fish but to human
life. From an angling, from an æsthetic, but most
of all from a sanitary point of view it is right that
we should preserve our streams from pollution
other than what is absolutely unavoidable. My
strong belief in this matter will, I hope, be regarded as a good excuse for repeatedly referring to
pollution in this little book.

To turn to a more pleasant subject, I should like
to say that I have not in the least degree changed
my opinion that a multiplicity of different kinds of
flies and patterns is unnecessary, so far, at any
rate, as the dry fly method of angling is concerned.
But I have found that views as to the necessity of
certain flies and patterns for certain streams are
held so firmly by many "local anglers," in regard
to wet fly fishing, that I have felt it only right and
fair to give lists of favourite flies and patterns for a
great number of waters in various parts of the
south country. For dry fly work the blue or olive
dun in its various forms and shades seems to hold
the field as the best of all lures for the trouting
season as a whole. It has, indeed, no serious rival
out of the brief May-fly season.

G. A. B. D.

CONTENTS

PART I.

CHAPTER I.

PART II.

CHAPTER I.

CONTENTS

CHAPTER IV.

CHAPTER V.

CHAPTER VI.

CHAPTER VII.

CHAPTER VIII.

CHAPTER IX.

CHAPTER X.

LIST OF ILLUSTRATIONS

Nos. 2, 3, 4, 6, 7, 8, 9 *are from photographs taken by H. P. Robinson and Son, Redhill.*

THE SOUTH COUNTRY
TROUT STREAMS

PART I

CHAPTER I

SOUTH COUNTRY ANGLING

IT is a somewhat curious fact that a trout-fishing expedition or holiday commonly conveys the idea to the south country man, and more especially perhaps to the Londoner, of a trip to the north of England, to Wales or Scotland, or even much further afield to the streams and lakes of Scandinavia. Devonshire, it is true, is widely known and recognised as a trout-fishing county, but, setting that single county aside, one may say that the south and south-west parts of England are not usually thought of in connection with trout and trout fishing, as are the more northern parts of the country. Scotland is perhaps more generally regarded as the true home of the trout and as the natural resort of the trout fisherman than any other part of the United Kingdom ; and it is certain that Scotland contains—as, for the matter of that, so do

B

Ireland, Wales, and the Northern counties of England from Derbyshire to Northumberland—a great number of beautiful trouting waters. The southern counties do not contain nearly so many trout waters as those other parts of the country I have referred to ; and perhaps this may have a good deal to do with the notion that, south of, say, Derbyshire or Yorkshire, England is not a land of trout streams—this and the fact that fly fishing for trout, salmon, and grayling has come to be associated in many minds with more romantic scenes than the counties which this little work will deal with can boast ; with the wild moorlands and uncultivated districts, and with the pure strong air of the mountains.

We have less streams in the south, and as for lakes we have practically none ; but, for all that, I do not in the least hesitate to assert that a good deal of the finest trout fishing in the United Kingdom is actually in or hard by the counties or shires of the southern seaboard.   Some of it is within three hours of the heart of London, by which I mean that a man, if he has the right to fish and the time and desire, may leave his home within a mile or two of one of the great London railway stations after a moderately early breakfast and before midday be angling in the purest and sweetest of genuine trout streams.   He can accomplish the feat in two hours inclusive in a certain number of cases ; and, in a very few, perhaps well within that space of time.   The trout of some portions of the Cray are, alas, as extinct almost as the salmon of the Thames, once so dreaded by the apprentices of London, the wild fowl of Pimlico Marshes, or the woodcock that old-time sportsmen

hoped to flush near where now stands Regent
Street or the Marble Arch. The Ravensbourne and
its trout are flowing away into history as the
Fleet or the Tyburn have long since done ; but
the " silver Wandle " of Pope's day has to some
extent withstood till now in its upper parts " the
wreckful siege " of bricks and mortar ; the Darenth
of Kent, if sorely tried by mill and tapped by
water company, has stood out well against builder
and polluter alike ; while the quiet flowing streams
of that charming trouting county Hertfordshire,
should at least see out us and our time. A smaller
space than the two hours above mentioned will often
suffice to find the keen angler at work on the banks
of any of these trout streams round about London.
If only we had more streams in the south of
England, and if they were more easily accessible—
for trout fishing in the south is not, it must be admitted, to be had by every angler for the trouble of
applying—we might be visited far more than we
are by eager anglers from all parts of the country
and many parts of the world. Ours indeed, if a
small, is a goodly angling heritage.

In succeeding chapters I shall try to describe
the beauties, the characteristics, and the variety of
angling in the south and south-eastern and western
counties, and later on to give in something like
detail short accounts of the fish, flies, peculiar
features and methods of angling in regard to each
leading trout stream. Before entering into these
particulars it will be well to treat in a broader and
more general way the subject of fish and fishing in
the south country as a whole.

Trout are, as we all know, occasionally found in
sluggish and dirty waters, such as canals, and in

slow deep streams which are naturally regarded as the proper homes of pike, perch, bream, barbel, and other coarse fish. They are also to be occasionally killed in more or less polluted running waters, provided the pollution be not of the poisonous kind resulting from mines or the manufacturers' mill. Such waters as these latter will not come into the scope of this little volume. There are certain features which are, I think, generally regarded as indispensable before a water can be fairly described as a trout stream. The good trout stream contains pure sweet water, with a gravelly or a rocky bed, with a current sufficient to save it—except of course in parts—from the reproach of being dead or sluggish, with shallows for the fish to spawn upon, and with green fresh-looking weed which affords cover for the fish and marks the spots where not a little of their food is placed by nature. The more perfect these features the finer the trout stream.

Clearness or sweetness of water is a feature of the trout stream which all trout fishermen, whether they hail from north or south, or fish with wet or dry fly, will agree is essential to perfection. The strength of the current is another matter. The north country angler and the believer in wet fly are more likely to set store by a pure trout stream which travels with plenty of life and sound, and so will he who affects the waters, moorland and others, of Devonshire and Somerset; while on the other hand the dry-fly angler desires to see in his perfect trout stream nothing like impetuosity; his is the favourite water which steals or gently sings its way through an undulating land. The good trout stream may, in fact, be either slow or swift flowing. I should say that the Barle of Somerset, and the Test of Hampshire, are both perfect trout streams in their widely different ways. Two more widely differing trout streams it would be impossible to name; and this brings me, by a natural enough transition, to the subject of the diverse modes of angling which must be put into practice by the fisherman who desires to feel at home on the trouting waters generally of the south.

The methods of angling for trout in the south are perhaps fewer in number than those of the north. We nowhere, I fancy, practise what is known on the Borders as creeper or stone-fly fishing—an interesting and exciting pursuit it must be—and the use of the natural May-fly which is still resorted to a good deal in certain Derbyshire waters and elsewhere, is now with us practically unknown. Fishing with the artificial minnow is far commoner in the north than in the south, and so is Stewart's extremely skilful style of worm fishing up stream in dry hot weather, when the water is too low for sport with the fly. The south country methods of angling for trout may be set down as three in number,—namely, wet fly, dry fly, and artificial minnow. Worm fishing by the coarse methods may, no doubt, be resorted to now and again by casual and unambitious anglers; but it frequently happens that trout taken with a worm are taken by pure accident—that is, the angler has baited his hook far more in expectation of securing some so-called coarse fish than with the deliberate intention of trout fishing. Stewart's scientific method of deliberately fishing for trout with a worm is a very different thing; but, as I have said, that method is not often practised in the south. In the case indeed of the great majority of the south country trout streams, east of Devonshire, "worming" in any form whatever is not commonly regarded as a legitimate style of angling. The rules of the chief clubs and associations on the chalk streams of Hampshire, Hertfordshire, and Kent, strictly forbid the use of any lure save the artificial fly, and in some cases the artificial fly does not in-clude the notorious and—as some anglers allege —most deadly Alexandra. The same rule is laid down by the owners of many private fisheries; and all anglers are expected to rigidly adhere to it. Of course, it happens that here and there proprietors and leesees of waters not over well preserved are careless in these matters, and do not trouble to conform to what has certainly be-come a recognised custom among sportsmen on the chalk streams; while other instances occur where certain folk, who think perhaps more of the booty than of the sporting sentiment, having what are called commoner rights, will not think twice about worming in the most delicate dry-fly water. But, so far as the regular trout streams are con-cerned, this class is a small and not a very growing one.

In addition to the two ordinary methods of angling with the dry and the wet fly, there is one branch of the latter which deserves particular notice, and that is fishing with one large sunk fly such as an alder or a Wickham over a "tailing" trout, or in rough water, or during a high wind when the dry fly is out of the question. I have long been convinced that this method is an art in itself, in which neither good wet nor good dry fly

fishermen are by any means of necessity well versed.
The best hand at using a single big fly in this way
that I have ever known happens to be good both
with the wet and the dry fly. I have seen him
kill his four-pound trout on a dry fly water and
his three or four dozen moorland troutlets, five or
six to the pound, with the same rare ease, skill,
and modesty. The big single fly is fished with a
long line, and it is absolutely necessary to impart
to it plenty of movement. It is worked very much
as is a grilse or salmon fly, and is usually most
effective in shallow water. The trout, if he be
" tailing "—that is, rummaging about in the weeds
for freshwater shrimp and other crustacea, with his
tail every now and then breaking the surface of
the stream—will often follow with a distinct wave.
If the rate of the fly's progress is abated the fish
inevitably perceives the mistake he has made, and
very likely in turning away to resume his shrimp-
ing operations sees something of angler, rod, or
line, and is gone in an instant. It is necessary,
therefore, to go on working the fly into one's own
bank—always fish down stream when angling in
this style—as though the trout were not following
at all.[1] One must never strike till one feels the
fish, otherwise it is quite likely he will not come
again. When a trout is seen "tailing" the angler
fishes over him, but in other cases the fly should be
cast under the far bank and worked down with the
stream into the near one in the manner described.
The method is most deadly when there is a heavy

---

[1] It is not wise to withdraw or cease working your fly
too soon whether a fish has or has not been observed.
Ovid's advice cannot be improved on—" *Semper tibi pendeat
hamus, quo minime credis gurgite piscis erit.*"

wind blowing, though I have occasionally killed a fairly good trout in this way on a calm day and in water ordinarily well adapted to the dry fly. What the trout take the alder or Wickham for when fished in this style it is not easy to say: it has often been said that they cannot very well take it for any natural insect in the *imago* or *sub-imago* stage in that it in no wise resembles or imitates any known fly. I should add that a large March brown dressed on a 1 to 4 hook is some-times quite as good as, or even better than, the large alder for this style of fishing. The method is a telling one on several of the Hertfordshire streams, such as the upper Lea and the Mimram. I should say it would kill good trout at times on the Hampshire chalk streams, too, and on waters like the Pang and Lambourne, as well as on many parts of the Kennet. On the Devon and Somer-set streams the ordinary wet fly style up or down stream is far preferable. Indeed, the big alder, Wickham, or March brown fished down stream as a sunk fly may almost be regarded as a dry fly water device, only practiced in a few southern counties. I have repeatedly tried it in the Derby-shire Wye, and never with the least degree of success.

The large fly dressed on hooks Nos. 1, 2, 3, 4, or even 5, is also used for late evening fishing on a good many trout streams east of Devonshire, and it then commonly takes the form of one of the species of the sedge fly. Some anglers use it as a wet or sunk fly, others as a dry one, and very deadly it occasionally proves among heavy trout, which rarely look at any winged insect in the day-time except during the short May-fly season. The

Test is the real home of the big sedge fly angler, though there are plenty of other streams where the lure can be tried with success. For dry-fly use the large red or brown sedge, as tried by Holland of Winchester and others, floats well enough, but the confirmed believer in paraffin usually prefers to anoint the fly with a little of his favourite liquid before sending it on its mission.

Writing of paraffin reminds me that dry-fly fishermen seem, from the quite heated discussions which have taken place of late on this matter, almost ripe for division into two schools, one consisting of ardent believers in the necessity of anointment, the other—the minority, I fancy —of profound sceptics! In trying, not long ago, to take up a middle position, the writer found himself in rather hot water. He still ventures to hold the view that the fly can be made to float and to kill without the oil, and that the labours of drying it in the air are by no means of a Herculean character; but at the same time he is ready to admit that it is often a relief to have a little bottle at hand. When enjoying—thanks to a most generous friend—some delightful sport among the upper Test trout last May-fly season, he stealthily drew from the kitchen lamp in the Crook and Shears at Bransbury. Some say that you must anoint with scentless paraffin, but there is nothing whatever in this. Scentless paraffin may be rather more pleasant to handle, but ordinary lamp paraffin will do for the Test trout, and therefore, it may be safely assumed, for those of all other streams. One plan is "to paraffin" your flies before you start from your fishing quarters, when you know what you are likely to use. A small application on the

wings or hackle will suffice for quite a couple of
hours' use. I have worked a paraffined May-fly
hard for half an hour or so, killed fish with it, re-
placed it in the fly case, using in its stead another
specimen, and several hours later have returned to
it and found no need for any fresh application of
the oil. The power of paraffin must have come as
a revelation to many anglers.

The chief artificial trout flies of the southern
counties may, perhaps, be divided into two groups,
one consisting of those patterns which are more or
less common to the chalk and the chalk and gravel
streams, the other of the patterns used on the more
impetuous waters, moorland and other, of Devonshire, Somerset, and Cornwall. To the former
belong the May-fly, olive and blue duns, pale watery
dun, iron blue dun, yellow dun, with their various
spinners or *imagines*, alder, sedges, grannom and
Welshman button ; to the latter, in addition to
duns and spinners, the famous blue upright and
even more famous March brown. The last-
named insect is not, so far as I can learn, a chalk
stream fly at all, though curiously enough it is
often used on such waters both as a wet and a
dry fly, with no small degree of success. Lately,
hearing of the March brown on the upper Lea, I
asked an angler, whose knowledge of that trout
stream is extensive and peculiar, whether he had
ever seen the natural insect there. He replied that
he had not seen it once in the course of more
than a quarter of a century's regular angling in
the stream. But there is a dainty little fly of the
Ephemeridæ order, which, until closely examined,
resembles pretty closely the March brown in all
save size. This is the turkey brown which

Ronalds treats as quite distinct from the March brown, but which others, including the writer, have confused for a while. I noticed this insect in sparse numbers on several trout streams last summer, including the Lea and the Test, and saw it once or twice taken by trout and dace. It is a chalk stream fly which the tiers might with advantage set to work to try and produce some really good imitations of. Angling one apparently hopeless afternoon last season on the Lea, I floated a March brown over a nice bit of ripple under the far bank. Hearing a footstep behind me, I took my eyes off the fly to see who had come up, when a heavy plunge recalled my attention in a second. " Did you happen to see him ? " I asked the keeper. " Yes, sir, distinctly ; a three pounder if an ounce," was the reply ; " I made sure you had him." It is quite conceivable that my March brown had been mistaken by this big trout—who took care not to come again—for the turkey brown which was on the water the same day. Mr. Halford points out in his " Dry-Fly Entomology" that the turkey brown has three *setæ*, while the March brown has only two. The grannom is chiefly associated with Test, Kennet, and Lambourne, where it is sometimes, during its short period of existence as a *sub-imago* in the spring, taken with eagerness by the trout. But from what I have heard from those who are thoroughly well acquainted with the insect, I should be inclined to describe it rather as a very well known than a highly important fly from the south country angler's standpoint. The female is conspicuous by the bunch of green eggs she carries at her tail. The blue-winged olive dun, another chalk stream insect—its *imago* being the oddly named sherry spinner—may be regarded in the same light, as may the little yellow May dun, or, as it is sometimes rather well named, little May-fly dun. I have seen the latter on various streams in north and south, but only once or twice in anything like abundance. Last season I saw a regular hatch of this beautiful insect, which is considerably larger than the ordinary yellow dun, and found a good Test trout rising at every one which came into a sort of little bower he was inhabiting. It was a cold dull evening just before the height of the May-fly season. Upon comparing notes with Mr. William Senior I found that he too had noticed a hatch of the same fly that day on the Itchen.

To turn to the second group of flies. The March brown is a regular Devon insect, and a more agreeable sight than a rise of the troutlets of this delightful county at a large hatch of the insect it would surely be difficult to imagine. It would scarcely be too much to say that on every length of every stream in Devonshire, if not of Cornwall and Somerset too, it is a standard fly throughout the earlier part of the season, possibly only surpassed in popularity by the blue upright. The artificial, or rather series of artificials known as the blue upright is, unlike the March brown, very little in demand among south country anglers outside the counties of Devon, Somerset, and Cornwall, though it is occasionally used on "dry fly waters" in Kent and Gloucestershire. There is no natural insect known as the blue upright, and there exists some difference of opinion as

¹ See page 144.

to what fly it is supposed to be an imitation of.

These two groups, it will be seen, do not include certain insects, such as the cow-dung fly, which are not really water flies at all, but occasionally get blown on to the stream against their inclination and habit. Reference indeed has only been made to the common water flies of the southern counties with their imitations. Some of them, especially perhaps the cow-dung fly, are by no means unimportant to the angler, and their imitations may not fairly be classed among the fancy patterns, such as the governor—which really cannot be taken by any trout, as some will have it, for a bee!—or the Wickham or peacock. At the same time their visits to the water are of a merely accidental and occasional character, and they scarcely claim notice in a work of this character.

There are three or four lures, besides those already mentioned, which cannot be quite overlooked in a work on Southern trout streams. The palmers—which I am inclined to think must be regarded as uncommon visitors to cur streams —are imitations not of flies at all in an *imago* or *sub-imago* state, but of various caterpillars. The fly books of few Devon or Somerset anglers will be without them as the season advances ; while a large red palmer used in the large fly method of angling on chalk or semi-chalk streams further east, is sometimes irresistible when offered to heavy trout. There is the coch-a-bonddu, which is supposed to be the imitation of a small beetle, chiefly confined to the three most western counties referred to in this book ; the black gnat, a summer insect common to the whole of the South, and a favourite with some dry fly fishermen despite its diminutive size and the impossibility of dressing a really good imitation of the natural fly ; the various species of the " fisherman's curses" or the "smuts," which are so often dreadfully appetising to trout of chalk and limestone streams, yet which are scarcely worth the attention of the practical fly tier owing to the smallness of the hooks on which they must be dressed ; the white *cænis*, tiniest of *ephemeridæ*, which Mr. Halford tells us he has never yet found in his autopsies of trout and grayling ; the several gay "flies" known as the bumbles, which are confined to grayling-land—that is, so far as this book is concerned, east of the Avon; and lastly the well-known coachman, which is an evening fly, but which some Devonshire anglers keep on their cast as a dropper the season through, all weathers and all hours. This last is now being used, too, by chalk stream anglers both for wet and dry stream work as an evening lure. I was tempted into buying a few with double hooks and double split wings last season, but they killed no trout. It is said that the trout takes the coachman to be a white moth. Considering how rarely moths, white or other, alight, or get driven upon the water, it seems remarkable that trout should take the coachman in so spirited a manner, and in the morning, too, as well as at night. It is indeed puzzling, as are so many other things connected with the *salmonidæ*. Sometimes just as one has come to the conclusion that the grown trout of the clear slow running stream is well informed to an an-noying degree in the matter of flies, that he can detect and will reject any but the most perfect imitation in colour, shade, and size of the olive dun, he proceeds to rise and suck in a fly which, in colour, shade, and size, is a most imperfect representation of that insect. Then, when trout after trout has helped to force one very near the conclusion that the most indifferent artificial is good enough, he proceeds to detect and reject all but the most perfect. It is rather humiliating, and may remind one of the great philosopher who towards the end of his life laid it down that all we knew for certain was that we knew nothing.

CHAPTER II

THE boast of Tennyson's brook

"For men may come and men may go,
But I go on for ever"

might seem a bold one for some of our trout streams to make to-day, at least for those which are gradually being closed in upon by inevitable brick and mortar progress ; by the builder, the manufacturer, and the water company. One need hardly go back to the time when Notting Hill was a forest and Finsbury a fen to trace the pleasant little river Tyburn flowing from its rise near the Swiss Cottage through Regent's Park in almost a line with what is now—New Bond Street ! Nor is the Tyburn the only stream that has "vanished tone and tint" from the map of England. Was there not the Fleet river, famed for its high banks, which took its rise at Hampstead ? and can you really recognise without an effort in the grimy and long since fish-less lower Wandle of to-day the "Wandsworth River" of which a writer in the first quarter of this century speaks, a river containing

"trouts and very large silver eels"? Passing over
Chelsea Bridge but now, and looking for the
thousandth time with interest on London's perhaps
most picturesque bit of scenery, on the grand old
church, and the irregular beauties of Cheyne Walk,
and the noble curve in the dark flowing stream that
bears crowded steamboat, and blackened barge
that almost matches the colour of its own water, I
tried to imagine what an evening scene there must
have been like in the time of old Best, and I entirely
failed. "When you go to angle at Chelsea," he
writes, "on a calm fair day, the wind being in the
right corner, pitch your boat almost opposite to the
church, and angle in the six or seven feet water,
where, as well as at Battersea Bridge, you will meet
with plenty of roach and dace." Those were days
when the fifth arch of Westminster Bridge marked
an excellent place for the angler to fix his boat at,
and when Twickenham was distinctly good for a
trout. The Ravensbourne might have been included among the south country trout streams at a
considerably later date : I fear I cannot include it
in my list of Kent rivers to-day.

But though a few streams have dropped out of
the list of our south country trouting waters, whilst
others are sorely beset, happily these are but in a
very small minority. The lost rivers of London
are not perhaps—from, at any rate, the trout fisherman's point of view—of great import. Of far
more gravity are the two questions of pollution
and want of water, which have of late years
threatened, if not actually destroyed, many an
excellent fishery. Several test cases in regard to
the evil of pollution have been tried within the
last ten years in regard to South of England

C

trout streams and the verdicts have been exactly as the angler would have wished. To single out two instances in point. There was the case of polluting the Darenth of Kent, close to Dartford, a deadly pollution by powder mills bleach which destroyed numbers of good trout, and the pollution of the Anton of Hampshire by Andover sewage, which made up in abomination what it may have lacked in deadliness. In both these cases the law was interpreted against the polluters, and as a consequence the Darenth trout still thrive and when hooked fight as game as most, while the Anton will again be sweet and pure.

Unfortunately it is not by any means always practical to prove an infringement of the Rivers Pollution Act of 1876, or to go to law at all. Pollution may be of a much more insidious and occasional character than in the cases just mentioned, and the evil may be more widely distributed and therefore much less easy to check by one decided blow. I candidly admit that the number of cases of fine trout streams in various parts of the south of England more or less polluted, which have come to my knowledge since I have undertaken this little work, has filled me with surprise. The Buckinghamshire Chess itself, which I always used to regard as one of the purest and least tainted of chalk streams, is not free from the reproach ; the peaceful little Hampshire Arle or Meon has not escaped ; while the Colne, long before it reaches the Thames, and where it still is—or should be—a genuine trout stream, has suffered and is suffering grievously. One is inclined to think that the deliberate poisoning or pollution of a trout stream is always a crime against nature as well as an

offence against man ; but there are degrees of
guilt, perhaps, in those who commit the sin. The
blackened rivulets that one so often sees in the
north and midlands are piteous spectacles ; but, at
any rate, they are the result of great works and
mills and manufactories which keep thousands of
hands busy and add to the wealth and prosperity
of the country. On the other hand the vandalism
of those slovens—be they private individuals or
public bodies—who shoot their semi-crude sewage
and rubbish into the running stream seems to have
not a redeeming feature ; I doubt if even Mr.
Ruskin could exaggerate the heinous character of
their misdeed. It might well be said, " Oh, their
offence is rank, it smells to Heaven."

To turn to the second of the serious evils that
threaten many of our pleasant fisheries in the
south of England. Shortness of water, in the case
both of the chalk and gravel streams, and of the
streams of the three western counties, Somerset,
Devon and Cornwall, which flow through land with
a sub-soil of rock and hard stone, is, of course,
frequently due to natural causes. The small
streams of Exmoor and Dartmoor always dwindle
down towards the latter part of summer, and the
volume of water in many of the lesser non-moor-
land streams is nearly always sadly diminished from
the same cause—want of rain—long before the
angling season is over. This failing in the supply
of water is, as we all know, not peculiar to the
streams of the south, but is common to rapid trout
streams in all parts of the world. The chalk
streams, depending entirely on springs, are not
affected by hot dry weather nearly so much as are
the more rapid waters referred to, though

ultimately they must be reduced, no doubt by shortness in the rainfall, probably in the following season. But both the rock and the chalk streams have been in many cases lowered of recent years by the operations of water companies. An angler whose experience and knowledge in regard to the chalk streams of the home counties are possibly unique—he has fished them for upwards of half a century, and has founded various angling clubs in several counties—tells me that he is absolutely certain that the springs of, for instance, some of the Hertfordshire and Kent rivers have been, and are being, surely and steadily lowered by the water companies. The chalk through which these rivers flow is like a great sponge. The water company proceeds not to exactly put its pipes into the river, but to extract the precious fluid from the chalk in the neighbourhood of the river, and in this way the springs are inevitably lowered. In other parts of the country the depredations of the water companies and of corporations are on a much more open and avowed scale. An owner of two very noted salmon fisheries in the west of England tells me that all his best water has been taken, so that angling with a fly is now a snare and a delusion. Has not Dartmoor itself been threatened? Even confirmed anglers will admit that water is desirable for other purposes besides that of fly fishing, but one doubts whether there are many people sufficiently philanthropic to regard with pleasure the tapping of their choice trout streams in the interests of the water company shareholder, and incidentally perhaps of humanity.

Another rather constant cause of indifferent sport in south of England streams in various counties is

the mill. On large streams like the Test, below
say Longparish, the mills scarcely harass the
angler or disturb the trout, but the case is different
where small streams are concerned. By holding
up the water in order to get a good store to work
with, that very picturesque person the miller,
white-dusted as the walls of his premises and
commonly blessed according to poets with a sweet
daughter, sorely tries the patience of the trout
fisherman. It is annoying to the fly fisherman who
arrives at the stream, eager for sport, to find the
water reduced to a mere trickle and the trout at
their wit's end to find shelter. In Kent and
Hertfordshire it is often one's lot to wait for a
matter of hours for the water, or to find a good rise
suddenly stopped by the operations of some mill
above. Moreover this constant interference with
the water by mills seem to have the effect in at
least some rivers of disturbing the trout and
making them disinclined to feed at the surface.
When the water, pent up for several hours, does
come down it brings with it a quantity of river
refuse and bottom food, of which the trout partake
freely to the discomfiture of the fly fisherman. The
lower the springs of the river the more necessary,
of course, the miller finds it to hold up the water
for working his wheel.

The miller is often a good fellow, who loves to
see a bit of sport, and will sometimes grant a
day's fishing to a keen angler; but still business is
business. I once, on a pretty little chalk stream,
struck an agreeable bargain with a sporting miller.
It was a summer day about May-fly time, and the
scene was by a delicious mill race in a land of
sleepy hollows. Mid-day found me hungry both for

sport, of which I had had none, and for luncheon, which I had quite forgotten to bring with me from town. The miller soon found out how matters stood and, disappearing for a little time into his floury regions, brought out some home made bread and cheese. A few minutes later he good-naturedly set his wheel going, and before long, there being a nice hatch of olive dun, I was able to repay my friend with a brace of fine trout. That was years ago, but whenever I find my way up to the mill the man comes forth from among his bulging sacks to watch the fun, and sometimes he will point me out a likely trout. It is certainly the spot of all spots to lunch at. About the race there always seems a chance of finding a good trout stirring even during the least likely part of the day, and there are often certain back streams and ditches which contain a particularly large fish in perfect condition. And then it is pleasant to sit down in the grass and watch

> " The sleepy pool above the dam,
>   The pool beneath it never still,
>   The meal-sacks on the whitened floor,
>   The dark round of the dripping wheel."

On the whole the small mill of the southern stream has its compensations for the angler, though it does sometimes interfere badly with the filling of his creel. Moreover, it is rarely an eyesore in the landscape.

Few questions in connection with the present condition and the future prospects of our southern trout streams are of more consequence than that of the scarcity of natural fly in many waters. The complaint of scarcity of fly is a common one in many parts of the country, and one frequently hears it in the north of England. In the case of the north, and also of the three most western counties referred to in this book, it is usually attributed to unseasonable weather. The insect is there all right, but simply has not hatched—such is the belief. The chalk stream angler, on the other hand, is often found lamenting that the fly is disappearing. He attributes it to the lowering of the springs of the river, to injudicious weed cutting, and to tampering over much with the water after the method of some very zealous keepers.

Pollution, a correspondent assures me, has had much to do with lessening the number of natural flies on the lower Colne of Middlesex ; only the " more hardy species," he writes, " having escaped." The fly has diminished for some reason or reasons in various waters ; but is the evil quite so widespread and growing as some would have us believe ? I ask the question because I have more than once heard anglers, and good ones too, complaining that there has been no fly out on a day when I have noticed, at a different part of the stream perhaps, a good number of insects of different species, flat-winged as well as upright. The story is certainly not a new one, and some who have not read that entertaining little book may be surprised to learn that Sir Humphry Davy in his *Salmonia*, published close upon seventy years ago, discusses it. " It appears to me that since I have been a fisherman, which is now the best part of half a century, I have observed in some rivers where I have been accustomed to fish habitually, a diminution of the number of flies." But curiously enough Sir Humphry did not notice this diminution in the case of the

chalk and gravel streams—such as those of Surrey,
Hants, and Bucks—but in other waters. He
attributed the evil to the cultivation of the country,
to the draining of bogs and marshes which fed
streams and in which the water flies and their larvæ
were so often to be found. I have myself been supplied with several instances of the May-fly greatly
diminishing in quantity in rivers and stretches of
rivers. In parts of the Dorsetshire Frome it has
sadly decreased, so that there can hardly be said to
be anything of a May-fly season on the Club water at
Dorchester nowadays. On the other hand it has
appeared on the head waters of the Lea in immense
numbers of late, and—to go outside the country
covered by the south country trout streams—on
the Derbyshire Wye it has been hatching in at
least equal profusion. Yet on the other hand on the
head waters of the Lea of recent years there has
been such a small quantity of the lesser *ephemeridæ*,
of those duns and spinners on which the chalk
stream angler chiefly depends, that the Hatfield
Fishing Club has just commenced the interesting
experiment of breeding water flies in addition to
young fish,—a most enterprising step, which perhaps other clubs afflicted with a scarcity of small
fly will be following presently. The experiment
of transplanting or introducing certain water flies
is not absolutely novel, though it has hitherto not
been attempted on a considerable scale. The late
Mr. Andrews told me that he had been successful
in introducing both May-fly and alder on his
beautiful fish ponds at Crichmere in Surrey, and
had had the pleasure of often seeing the big fish
compete eagerly for the insects when hatched.
Another fish culturist, Mr. Armistead, proprietor

of the Solway hatchery, actually suggests a
regular insectarium, if I may use such a barbarous
compound, and is quite convinced that the rearing
of water flies for angling purposes is practical. Considering how easy the rearing of *lepidoptera* is to
collectors, there certainly does not seem to be any
great obstacle to dealing with the *ephemeridæ* and
other families in the same way.

Pollution, water company operations, interference
by mills and shortness of fly—with, as a consequence, unwillingness of trout to rise freely at the
artificial—form the four chief standing grievances
of the south country angler of to-day, though I
must admit that I have heard, and sometimes
indulged in various others, the supposed results
of atmospheric and human shortcomings. Among
these four grievances, the water company is perhaps the newest, and in the not remote future it
may be the most serious of all. These angling
woes are rather dispiriting to dwell upon ; and
especially when they apply one and all to
the same water, as is sometimes the case, the
angler has reason indeed to complain. But
happily there are several features in connection
with trout fishing of to-day and trout fishing prospects which may fill us with hope for the future
of our pastime.

The increased number of anglers—which I cannot
profess, as an angling writer or an angler, to regard
with regret—and the ever-growing popularity of
fly fishing for trout, have led to the careful preservation and the improvement of many waters all over
the south of England. Trout fisheries, which
were formerly managed in the most happy-go-
lucky way, which were poached and overrun with

pike, are now well looked after and cleared from
time to time of coarse fish. The rents of good
stretches of fishing water have gone up greatly in
all parts of the country, and landlords hit hard by
agricultural depression have, in many cases, made
up some of their losses by letting their streams to
clubs, associations, and private individuals. A
hundred pounds a mile is by no means an unheard
of sum for chalk stream fishing in a first-class and
easily reached river where the trout run large.
Preservation leads to re-stocking, which is a feature
of the greatest possible importance from an angling
point of view. There are those who view re-
stocking with small favour, and would rather, so
they declare, bear the ills we have than fly to
others that we know not of. "Our old Lea fish
mayn't be beautiful," said a rare angler to me
recently, "but they shape far better than the fish
we have re-stocked with. I really think we should
have done better to leave it alone." That re-
stocking can be overdone few will deny who have
had experience of small waters packed with fish
which might reach a couple of pounds or so if they
had room, but which actually go out of condition
before attaining anything like that weight, and are
often found to be black and lanky even after the
may fly has come and gone. An over-stocked
small stream is indeed a rather pitiable sight.
Quite likely, too, my angling friend quoted above
was right in preferring an old native of the
Lea to any newcomer. It is hard to improve
on Nature's arrangements. But in these angling
days it is necessary to often supplement her
efforts, and hence trout culture has come to be
regarded as a great boon to fly fishermen. Some

clubs now have their own hatcheries, managed, of course, by the water-keeper in their employ- ment, and if the business is managed successfully they sometimes find that they have far more year- lings from time to time than they used. They are hence able to sell to other clubs and pro- prietors, and to make distinct profit. Few people now stock their waters with fry unless those waters are practically fishless, as otherwise hardly any will be able to escape their enemies or arrive at maturity.

Yearlings at from fifteen to twenty-five pounds a thousand, or even "two-year-olds" at from six to ten pounds a hundred, are much cheaper in the end than fry at, say, twenty-five shillings a thousand. There are already several well-known breeding establishments in the South of England —such as the Exe Valley hatcheries and the Crichmere ponds at Haslemere, in addition to some excellent private hatcheries. The Wilton Fly Fishing Club may be taken as a thoroughly enterprising one, and it is well to note what that Club has done in the way of stocking its ten miles of trout and grayling water since 1891. The stretch of water on the Wylye came into the hands of the Club in 1890, and the first thing to do was to clear the river as far as possible of the coarse fish, which were found to be very numerous. During the nine months ending 31st December, 1890, no less than 9,151 coarse fish were removed from the water. Out of this number over 2,000 were pike, many of which weighed over 10 lbs. In the following year the number of pike taken was 897 ; in 1892 the number was 517 ; in 1893 it was 103, and in 1894 it dropped as low as 23.

Stocking with common trout and the Loch Leven variety was carried on almost at once on an extensive scale, the Club putting in about 400 fish exceeding two years in age, 800 "two-year-olds," close on 6,000 yearlings, together with 45,000 fry of *Salmo fario* and ova and eyed ova. Over a thousand grayling, composed partly of yearlings and partly of sizable fish, and 35,000 grayling ova were also introduced. Whether the introduction of the grayling was wise may be a moot question. In some rivers they are far too numerous to suit the trout fisherman. A good many of us are not greatly devoted to the fish, which cannot be regarded as the equal of the trout ; but, all the same, it must be conceded that there are rivers in the south, notably the Test and Itchen, where grayling fishing is, during the autumn and winter months, a highly popular pastime among some of the best and keenest trout fishermen. In any case I rather question whether a great percentage of those 35,000 ova reached maturity in such a stream ; they were probably found very good eating by their elders. Not every Club can stock its waters on this scale, but most can do a little from time to time, and a few hundred good yearlings in a mile or so of water free of pike will soon yield sport.

A good many attempts have been made within the last few years to acclimatise *Salmo fontinalis*, the American brook trout, or, more correctly, char, in our southern streams, but with no success, so far as I have heard. The fish mysteriously disappears, nobody knows for certain where, though the presumption is it goes down to the sea. Our streams, possibly by reason of their temperature, do not seem to be fitted to this most beautiful fish, nor have attempts to acclimatise the equally beautiful *Salmo irideus*, the rainbow trout, in rivers been successful. Two cases only of *fontinalis* and *irideus* being taken by anglers in south of England streams have been brought to my notice. The Duke of Bedford favours me with a statement to the effect that both *fontinalis* and *irideus* have been taken with the artificial fly on the Chess in Buckinghamshire, a most interesting fact.[1] The second instance is not quite so satisfactory, since my informant says he cannot be absolutely sure of the species of the fish he took from the head waters of the Lea ; but he believed, and still believes, that the trout from its great brilliancy and dissimilarity from the Lea fish and from Loch Levens could have been no other than a char.

Trout culture may, I suppose, be almost described as still in its infancy in this country, and it is practically only within the last thirty years or so that much alteration has been paid to it for angling purposes. We are believed to be considerably behind the Germans as pisciculturists, and to lose far more young fish than they do during the process of rearing. But if trout fishing continues to increase in favour as it has been doing during within the last twenty-five years or so, the rearing of fish is sure to become more and more general and to make strides. Some carefully preserved private waters of the south like the Chess, where the conditions are excellent for spawning, where there are no pike, and where anglers do not swarm, need no re-stocking ; and in such waters it might

---

[1] I have myself caught *fontinalis* in the Chess.—ED.

be unwise to introduce yearlings. It is very different with club, hotel, and ticket waters, which are very much fished ; there re-stocking is year by year an increasing necessity. . I am convinced that on trout culture the fate of the fly fisherman of the south of England will in the future depend very largely. As to the contention that trout artificially reared on minced horseflesh and other food used at the breeding establishments are not likely to rise so well at the fly as wild fish, it is not one that can be allowed for a moment to weigh against the great benefits conferred on the angler by trout culture. That artificially reared trout of, say, two years old, fed almost entirely off horsemeat mash, may if turned into a brook rise less regularly at May-flies or March browns than the fish reared by Nature, and may prefer grosser food—that this is a not unreasonable contention may well be admitted. In *The Book of the Dry Fly* (page 81) it is suggested that this may possibly be one of the causes of "the greater reluctance of the trout to take the fly" in some waters. The possible evil, however, cannot be set against the certain good ; and I for one be- lieve in the day when hundreds of miles of water in the south of England now neglected will be con- verted by stocking into excellent trout streams. To the south Country angler of the future will be denied the rare delight of falling in with a piece of long-overlooked water in which trout are few and leviathan-like ; but, on the other hand, there will surely be open to him by club, subscription, lease, or hotel or season ticket, many excellent stretches of water that are at present almost unworthy the notice of the fly fisherman. We may be pessimists

THE WEY AT EASHING.

after several days' hard angling in a chalk or rocky stream unrewarded by the smallest bit of sport, and may dwell with gloom on the deterioration of trout fishing in the south of England ; we should be optimists when we think of the progress which is being made in the science of pisciculture and of the well-stocked streams of the future.

CHAPTER III

THE south country trouting waters might be
roughly divided into two broad classes,—the first
consisting in the main of chalk and partly chalk
streams, flowing in the counties of Kent, Middlesex,
Sussex, Surrey, Hants, Herts, Bucks, Berks, Wilts,
and Dorset, and the second of the hard stone, rock,
and limestone streams which predominate in
Somerset, Devon, and Cornwall. But very striking
are the contrasts between many streams belonging,
so far as their origin is concerned, to the same
class. The Barle of Exmoor Forest and the Lyn
of North Devon are both rock-bound streams, but
they offer in their scenery a very vivid contrast.
At and above Simonsbath, where is Exmoor Forest
proper as distinct from the far larger tract commonly usurping the name, the Barle flows through
an almost treeless and desolate country, very
different from the sheltered and beautfully wooded
little gorge through which the Lyn, almost its
neighbour, rushes, often in white haste, to St.
George's Channel. Scarcely less striking is the contrast between the Chess of Buckinghamshire and the

Test of Hampshire, both flowing through the chalk, and both enjoying among their special admirers the reputation of being "the best trout stream in the south of England." Of course it must be admitted even by the most patriotic southerner that we have in our country none of the noble river scenery that is so plentiful in wild Wales and in the north. We have nothing that answers to the Welsh Dee or Usk ; and I do not think that any Devon man who knows the Derbyshire and Staffordshire waters will claim for his "delicious land" a stream of such invariable nobility in regard to its scenery as the Dove. The truth is we have hills where the northerner has mountains ; therein lies the secret of the superiority of the North of England, of Wales, and of Scotland, in point of grandeur of river scenery. Nor have we, with two notable exceptions, the splendid moor-lands which are a feature of so many northern rivers : we can only boast commons and here and there a so-called waste So much may be admitted ; but no more.

It may be hard, in writing of the beauties of the chalk streams in mid-June or in the declining days of summer to escape the charge of being a drawer of the long bow. But at any rate one may draw it in good company ; for what says Charles Kingsley, not in his *Chalk Stream Studies*, but in *Yeast*, of these waters ? "Of all the species," he writes, "of lovely scenery which England holds, none, perhaps, is more exquisite than the banks of the chalk rivers." Chalk stream pictures are artfully inserted into more than one page of *Yeast*. Launcelot sits and watches the stream for hours, and this is what he sees :—" The great trout with

D

their yellow sides and peacock backs lunged away
in the eddies, and the silver grayling dimpled
and wandered among the shallows, and the may
flies flickered and rustled round him like water
fairies with their green gauzy wings; the coot
clanked musically among the reeds; the frogs
hummed their ceaseless vesper-monotone; the
kingfisher darted from a hole in the bank like a
spark of electric light; the swallows' bills snapped
as they twined and hawked above the pool; the
swifts' wings whirred like musket balls as they
rushed past his head; and ever the river fleeted
by bearing his eyes away down the current, till its
wild eddies began to glow with crimson beneath
the setting sun." It is a scene such as most
anglers who know any of our chalk streams have
witnessed and gloried in at May-fly time. It was
not the Hampshire Test, I fancy, which Kingsley
had in mind when writing this description; but it is
perhaps in some of the upper reaches of that
perfect river that the chalk stream scenery most
absolutely fascinates the lover of nature as well as
of angling. When the springs are full and the
meadows and commons in many places, even at
some little distance from the stream, have a way
of unpleasantly reminding too slenderly shod
anglers and searchers after nature's treasures of
this abundance of water, then is the time in fine
weather to see the summer Test at its fairest; then
and sometimes a little later, too, in July and early
August, before the season shows the least signs of
decay.

The more water there is in the marshy places
by the river side, the more greenery and the greater
wealth of insect, bird, and plant life. It has

always seemed to me, from birdsnesting days
down to the present time, that the most interesting
flowers and some of the most interesting insects,
and not a few of the most interesting birds are to
be found in places too often—or should I say
fortunately often ?—inaccessible save to the man
who is so clad as to be able without discomfort to
go up to or above his knees in water.

By the banks of the Test the water rail, the
kingfisher—neither bird I am happy to think, so
rare in the south of England as sometimes
supposed—the wild duck, the snipe, the yellow
wagtail, and the reed warbler are all to be found
breeding in spring and early summer; and it
would surely be hard to name a group of more
interesting and beautiful birds than these species
form when taken together. Of course this little
group is very far from including all the birds which
are constantly to be found about the banks of the
chalk stream in the nesting season. The stream,
or the splendid wealth of vegetation about it,
draws a large number of our most familiar resident
and migratory species. From source to sea the
pure chalk stream is teeming with bird life, and
loud during a portion of the summer with bird
language ; nightingales in every coppice, thicket,
and hedgerow by the stream ; sedge-warblers never
silent while the daylight lasts, and sometimes
inclined to be noisy after it has faded away ;
corncrakes, wherever there is a thick crop of
meadow grass, with note unlovely perhaps when
considered, but somehow never wearisome ; demon-
strative moor-hens and undemonstrative dabchicks
or little grebes closer in among the tangle of the
river banks, and especially in creeks and bye

streams, into which the angler-naturalist grown
incautious may sometimes find himself sinking far
more than knee deep ; cuckoos here and there and
everywhere incessantly answering one another from
woods and clumps of elms on opposite sides of the
water ; swallows skimming up and down the river,
too often more eager than the trout for the rise of
small fly—these are a few of the many feathered
creatures which the chalk stream draws to itself.

In the rich soil of the miles upon miles of
meadow land, which is watered not only by the
main stream and its fascinating branches and
tributaries and dykes—dykes, mind you, that
sometimes hold their four-pound trout—but also
by artificial feeders, there is a splendid array of
flowers, from the time of the "cowslip wan" of
April to that of the yellow loosestrife of August.
Fishing some famous shallows from an islet in
the Test towards the end of last August, I looked
up stream while waiting for a rise and saw a sight
on that calm afternoon that will not easily be
erased from the memory.   One branch of the
stream, crystal clear, fit for slaking the thirst on a
hot day, came gliding swift but unbroken over
emerald green weeds and clean gravel, on which a
trout could here and there be distintly seen
resting.   On the islet formed by this branch and
the main stream, an islet not less lovely than that
lawny one that lives in Shelley's lyric, was a mass
of colour and variety which baffles all description.
There were tall graceful ash trees slightly inclining
over the water as though to catch their portraits in
nature's looking glass, and willows always so thirsty
for the wave, and in the midst of the islet small
oaks, which had kept their freshness longer than

the trees of the great wood hard by—Harewood
Forest, Wherwell, or "Horrel" as it is locally called
—and darker alders nearer the stream. Then in
the front of all, even of the moist trunks of the
willows, there was a tall hedge of water plants.
Purple loosestrife prevailed in quantity among the
blossoms ; but the brilliant yellow loosestrife, one
of the handsomest flowers that grows in marshy
spots, claimed greater attention ; and in sheer bulk
of bloom, though scarcely in beauty, the great hemp
agrimony was easily foremost—these and other less
striking flowers all packed and pressed together
with aromatic water mints, with sedges, rushes, and
the river-loving grasses. The branch was on my
right, while the main stream, here more broken
than usual, hurried round the left side of the islet
and presently formed the splendid shallows.

Standing about the same place earlier in the year
before this great mass of green had reached its
prime, you might just see the toned-down red brick
walls and the latticed windows of the fishing cottage
on the bank of the main stream, with the thatched
fishing hut hard by. A perfect picture this, if
one could only paint it in words, and one out of
hundreds equally beautiful to be seen on a summer
day by the banks of most of our trout streams of
the south.

Many a day spent by the angler in this land
of chalk may be fishless, despite his skill with
the rod ; but few days which offer to him no fresh
delight for eyes, ears and mind. Even in the
absorbing time of the May-fly there are intervals
when the angler may turn his attention to what is
going on outside the stream, as well as within
it. One day in early June I came upon the pretty

butterfly called the greasy fritillary (*Artemis*) on
the banks of the Test, as others have found it in
numbers in certain water-meadows of the little
Chess of Buckinghamshire ; another, upon the
retiring water rail, feigning, it seemed, for the
sake of eggs or young, to be badly injured ; whilst
one evening later on in the season my search for
scarce water flowers, " far through the marish green
and still " was well rewarded by the discovery of
some fine specimens of that curious escape from
cultivation, *Mimulus*, with fine yellow blossoms
spotted with rich brown. A chalk stream diary
might be well worth keeping. How the perusal
of it would lighten the gloom of some dark winter
day in the roaring city ! Even for those busy folk
who have neither time nor taste for the countless
details, which make up a southern trout river scene,
there is a beauty that soothes and satisfies about
the very green meadows and the gently undulating
country of the Test. " It is not," wrote a gifted
descendant of Colonel Hawker of Longparish, " the
scenery men cross continents and oceans to admire,
and, yet it has a message of its own. I felt it that
day when I was heart weary and was glad that
in one corner of this restless world the little hills
preached peace."

Not a few of the old-world hamlets of, for
instance, the Test at Itchen deserve the name of
fishing villages. For the sake of a day or two on
a renowned trout stream, keen anglers, even out
of holiday time, will tear themselves away from the
world of " getting and spending " and come down
on Thursday evening to fish Friday and Saturday.
Ah ! those week-ends, when the weather holds
up and the fish rise to the fly ! There is a rare

fragrance about the little angling inn or cottage
with its garden of flowers and vegetables, a medley
of ornament and use. What angler has not noted,
on his evening drive to the village from this quiet
countryside station, the incense of the hedgerows?
The may has gone perhaps, but there is fragrance
none the less; for in these refreshing spots sweet
odour seems to succeed sweet odour the spring
and summer through. After dinner or supper the
visitor must go out, though it is growing quite dark,
to inspect what he can of the river he is to fish next
day ; and should it happen that there is that most
seductive of all angling things, an evening rise,
he will be devoting an extra hour on his return to
his village quarters to overhauling and preparing
tackle against the morrow's sport. In the morning
he will wake before he is called, and throw open the
lattice to take a draught of that best of stimulants
—the fresh morning air of the country, and to hear
a portion of "some wild skylark's matin song."

Some one has declared that the chief pleasure in
angling is to be found in the preparations for
angling. This is, of course, an exaggerated way
of putting it ; but the beauty of the landscape and
the sweetness of his quarters,—who would deny that
these things, at any rate, are material to the
angler's complete content? The fishing quarters
where "the landlady is good and kind," and where
the sheets smell of lavender, have been precious
since the days of Walton. "It is worth while,"
wrote Mr. Froude, "to spend a few days at Cheneys,
if only for the breakfast—breakfast on fried pink
trout from the Chess, fresh eggs, fresh yellow butter,
cream undefiled by chalk, and home-made bread
untouched with alum." But let no one suppose

from these words that the historian was a casual
angler, a man who merely made a fly rod an excuse for a little rest and change ; on the contrary
he was an ardent fly fisherman.

It is a far cry from the chalk streams of Hampshire or Hertfordshire to the moorlands of Devon
and Somerset, from the two or three pound trout
to the five or six to the pound troutlet, and there
are probably some regular home county anglers to
whom such sport as Erme or Okement, Barle or
upper Exe could offer, would seem scarce worth
having. I do not think, however, that the great
majority of good anglers who have been accustomed to sport among the heavy fish of the chalk
streams will quite fail to appreciate the pleasures of
the different kind of fly fishing that is associated
with Princetown or Simonsbath. The season for
these moorland troutlets of the Western Counties
opens much earlier than that for most of the rivers
within a hundred miles or so of London. February
is scarcely an inviting month to the angler, but the
fish of the moorland streams are often fit for the
creel then, while March sometimes turns out to be
the best month in the year. As the summer draws
on, the streams, which, unlike those of the chalk
country, are directly and immediately affected by
the rainfall, often begin to dwindle, and the prospect
in July and August will then wear rather a hopeless
look.

When the east wind blows in March or early
April up in these high places of the south of England—as it has the habit of doing—and the snow
yet appears plainly enough here and there in great
white patches on the hillsides, it may seem like
angling in mid-winter. How widely different fly

fishing for moorland troutlets under these conditions to stalking the three-pounders by the banks of the Hampshire chalk streams on a soft June morning! different, but still delightful to the keen fly fisherman and the lover of nature in her sterner and more desolate aspects. On many an April day on the upper Barle or Exe or on the romantic Bagworthy water, I have fished from early morning to nightfall, till it has become so dark that I have no longer been able to see my cast of two or three flies on even the stiller and smoother stretches of the stream, and have at length turned homeward without by any means feeling that the day has been an overlong one. The moorland air is wonderfully bracing at about the season when the angling is often at its very best ; a finer nerve and brain tonic for a hard-worked man, provided he be robust enough to stand the bitter wind and the rough walking, it would be hard to find.

Up here in the wilds, even when the summer has come, there is little of the lavish bird, insect, and plant life which characterise the trout streams of the home counties. Nature has dealt out a comparatively "stinted stepmother dole of gifts" to the land of the rock and granite streams. High up and near the sources of these trout streams the dipper is one of the few birds that frequent bank and boulder, and the heather often the predominating, indeed almost the solitary, flower for miles and miles. You may occasionally flush a blackcock, and the partridge's cry where a little cultivation has been persevered with may tend to slightly soften the scene. But sternness and scantiness of life are as decidedly the features of the scenery of these moorland trout streams as softness and pro-

fusion of life are of the chalk streams. Long may
it remain so! Who would desire to see Dartmoor
under cultivation, or Simonsbath more than a little
shelter in the wilderness?

These moorland streams of Devon and Somerset
are, like the Cornish waters, quite sacred to the
trout. Coarse fish are here unknown, and the artificial fly is adhered to by the great majority of
anglers throughout the season. The fish run very
small, but they are extremely plentiful, full of
fight in their small way, and of exquisite beauty.
"Spots of cochineal," says Jefferies, "finely mixed
together dot his sides; they are not red nor yellow
exactly, but as if gold dust were mixed with some
bright red. A line is drawn along his glistening
greenish side, and across this are faintly marked
lozenges of darker colour, so that in swimming
past he would appear barred. There are dark
spots on the head between the eyes, the tail at
its lower and upper edges is pinkish, his gills
are bright scarlet. Proportioned and exquisitely
shaped he looks like a living arrow formed to
shoot through the water. The delicate little
creature is finished in every detail, painted to
the utmost minutiæ, and carries a wonderful store
of force, enabling him to easily surmount the
rapids."

A long spring day devoted to filling a little creel
with two or three dozen troutlets in the land of the
wild red deer and the black grouse, or among the
sparkling streams of Cornwall, is not one to be
easily forgotten by the angler accustomed to more
luxurious forms of sport. The lights of his inn are
very welcome to the angler after a long trudge
home over a rough country; such a day's sport

means fatigue, but it means also a good appetite and a sound sleep. I have referred to the Cornish trout streams because there is reason to believe they are underrated by many anglers. They run very low at times ; but when there is water there are trout of from four to six or seven to the pound to be taken with fly in scores of small, even un- named, streams in that pleasant land. Some of these Cornish streams are perfect trout waters in their miniature way. Wandering about the country on foot for a short time in the winter recently I came upon some streams, hidden away in the woods and among the great boulders, that set me longing for the return of the fly-fishing season. After a long walk in snow and bitter wind over the wilds of those fine downs called Goonhilly—the serpen- tine district of Cornwall and the home of that scarce and beautiful heather *Erica vagans*—I found myself by chance in a little sheltered lane near Helston, by which ran the prettiest rivulet imagin- able, a feeder probably of the Cober stream. Hidden away deep down among the strange dwarfed-looking oaks, the brambles, and the mis- cellaneous and very small timber which make up a Cornish lane, it might have seemed incapable of holding even fish of the size of the Barle ; and yet I had the delight before long of seeing several trout of four or so to the pound dart up stream. It would require skill in stalking and fine tackle to take trout out of such water as this ; and I was not surprised to hear that some good Cornish anglers use only one fly on their cast. With a nine-foot rod and the finest gut such angling might be quite scientific.

Inclination bids me dwell upon the beauties and

attractions of other trout waters in the South of
England, besides the two classes—namely, the
major chalk streams and the moorland streams of
the two western counties, Somerset and Cornwall
—which we have just considered ; but the feeling
that it needs the hand of a master indeed to describe all the delicate details of the scenery of these
little rivers of ours, urges me in an opposite direction.   Otherwise it would be hard to pass over
the clear swift Coln of Gloucestershire, and the
happily named Windrush of the same county,—
streams not belonging to the chalk, but combining
some of the advantages and beauties of that class
of water with those of a more rocky bed.   Neither
could I here refrain from dwelling upon the Wiltshire and Berkshire Kennet, a noble trouting name
to conjure with among fly fishermen all over the
land : nor the excellent streams of Hertfordshire,
such as the Mimram or Maran, that can often
hide itself behind a thin hedge so as to be neither
seen nor heard by one who passes by within a
few yards, and knows nothing of its dashing two-
pounders ; and the baby Lea, where it emerges
from the Bedfordshire border to soon hold three,
yes, and four pounders, by pretty Wheathampstead and by Brocket, with its old brick walls and
noble timber.   The very names of these places are
alluring to the angler : he thinks of them in connection with villages half lost amidst towering
elms and wide-spreading horse-chestnut trees ;
graceful church spires; old inns held together by
many oak beams within and without ; and mills
whiter perhaps than even the little places of worship
dotted here and there above the blue Norwegian
fjords.

THE KENNETT, SAVERNAKE.

PART II

CHAPTER I

THE KENT STREAMS

KENT is scarcely a well-watered county from the fly fisherman's point of view, containing, now that the Cray has been all but lost to the angling world, only three trout streams of note,—namely, the Stour, the Little Stour, its tributary, and the Darenth. There is a streamlet at Dover, the Dour,[1] and there are also trout here and there in the tributaries or branches of the Medway, the chief river of the county, setting aside, of course, the Thames; but these hardly claim notice, being of an insignificant character. The Dour does

[1] This is one of the most significant of English river names, carrying us back to the days when the population of Kent was Celtic. The name Dour almost certainly represents the old Celtic *dur*, water, a contracted form of *dobhar* (dovar), which remains unchanged as Dover. Although *dobhar* and *dur* no longer exist as terms signifying "water" in modern Celtic dialects, the old word may still be traced in the Gallic for "otter"—*dōran*, the water beast—and in the Welsh *dyfrgi*, Breton *durki* and Irish *dobharchu*, the water dog. Other Celtic names for rivers survive in Avon, Exe, Ouse, Loddon and Dublin on the Test.—ED.

contain trout ; but it is only a few miles in length
from source to sea. Kearsney is perhaps the best
place for the angler who has permission to fish to
stay at. As regards the upper parts of the
Medway which contain trout, East Grinstead
may be mentioned, and Headcorn, on the stream
called the Beult. There are plenty of coarse
fish lower down the Medway, but no trout. The
river is not, indeed, adapted to the *Salmonidæ*
save here and there in its head waters.

The Stour, the biggest of the Kent trout streams, is
forty-five miles in length. It flows through the east of
the county, rising about fifteen miles north-
west of Ashford, and entering the sea at
a point about seven miles from Sandwich. It was
described by Skrine, in his *Principal Rivers of
Great Britain*, as a very circuitous stream. "The
Stoure," he says, "after leaving Ashford, traverses
a sweet vale," a statement which certainly holds
as good to-day as it did in the early part of the
century. Best, who wrote at about the same
period, included the Stour among the four most
famous trout streams ; the others being the Kennet
near Hungerford, the Wandle near Carshalton,
and the Amerly in Sussex, the last named of
which must surely have sadly deteriorated within
the last century if Best were correct in his estimate.
He also stated that "the Stower" was reputed
to breed "the best trout in the south-east of England," at which there is perhaps not much to
cavil. The best trouting on the Stour at present
is not in the upper reaches, but between Wye
and Canterbury, though there are trout mixed
with coarse fish between the former place and
the source of the stream, as well as in a feeder
which rises near Westenhanger station, and after

a ten miles' course joins the Stour by Ashford. Mr. Pike, of Maidstone, who has stocked a good deal of Kent water with trout, and has a long and intimate knowledge of the various streams, writes to me with enthusiasm of the Stour. He describes it as "a magnificent trout stream," and as holding "some very big fish." "Trout run," he says, ' quite 1½ lbs. average, and during the May-fly season big fellows of four and five pounds are to be had. Fish are very shy, and the dry fly is necessary. Three or four brace is a good day, but more are sometimes creeled." Among the principal owners of the fishing are Lord St. Vincent, of Godmersham Park, and Captain Hardy, of Chilham Castle, who has a fine stretch of the stream, and occasionally gives permission on the strength of a sufficiently good introduction. Formerly the tide flowed up as high as Fordwich, where the stream is now rather sluggish and muddy, and where there are a certain number of heavy fish. Six miles lower down, at Grove Ferry, the water becomes brackish, rising and falling with the tide ; and a friend tells me that near here there are a few large fish which turn their heads up or down according to the flow of the tide. It is easy to believe that they are very difficult to take with an artificial fly.

The Fordwich trout was formerly believed to be a distinct species of the family *Salmonidæ*, and Walton had some strange tales to tell about this fish. "You are to know," he says to Venator, "that this trout is thought to eat nothing in the fresh water,"—a statement[1] which some much

---

[1] On this interesting subject, see the latest report of the Fishery Board for Scotland, published in the spring of 1898.

more modern anglers have made in respect to
the salmon : and again, " Sir George Hastings,
an excellent angler, now with God . . . hath
told me he thought *that* trout (*i.e.*, the only Fordwich trout ever captured by our angler) bit not
for hunger but wantonness ; and it is rather to be
believed because both he, them, and many others
before him, have been curious to search into their
bellies, what the food was by which they lived ;
and have found out nothing by which they might
satisfy their curiosity." Another old angling
author writes of the Fordwich trout as differing
from all others " in many considerables, as greatness, colour, cutting white instead of red when in
season, not being takeable with an angle, and
abiding nine months in the sea, whence they
observe their coming up almost to a day." The
long and short of these fish stories is that the old
writers confused the brown trout with the sea
trout and possibly the grilse, which ascended the
Stour in due season. The famous " Fordwich
trout," which to this day some people are half inclined to believe in, no doubt was, and indeed still
is, either one or the other of these sea-going fish.
Probably many more sea trout and grilse ascended
the Stour formerly than at the present time ; but
both species are still taken by nets in the estuary of
the river near Pegwell Bay, and Mr. Pine informs me
he believes he has seen some as high as Fordwich.
The Stour, after passing Minster and Sandwich,
flows to the North Sea through wide marshes, where
flourish the great reed grasses used for thatching
and even fencing [1]—a wild and desolate region.

[1] Out of the Test rushes a useful and beautifully finished-
off basket is made in the neighbourhood of Longparish.

There are two associations on the Stour, the Lower Stour Fishery Association and the Upper Stour Fishery Association. The Lower Stour Association has been in existence for about six years, and its rights in regard to its three miles of water are vested partly in the corporation of Canterbury and partly in the landowners. The association throws open half the waters which it protects to the public and reserves the remaining portion as a subscription water,—entrance fee four guineas, and annual subscription four guineas. The water is well cleared of pike, and restocked every year with about a thousand two-year-old trout. The Upper Stour Fishery is treated in the same way.

The trout season is from April 1 to September 15, and fly and minnow are the two baits allowed. The flies commonly used on the Stour, which is a genuine chalk stream, are the olive, blue, and yellow duns, ginger quill, alder, red spinner, black gnat, and sedges. The May-fly is abundant on the upper part of the stream. Mr. Pike specially recommends two fancy flies, the governor and the pink Wickham, together with the blue upright. No trout can be killed on the association water of under thirteen inches in length. Chilham—Alma and Woolpack Inn—or Canterbury may be made headquarters by the angler according to whether he is fishing the upper or the lower part of the Stour.

The Little Stour rises near Bishopsbourne—of which the theologian Hooker was once rector—in the grounds of Bourne Place. "The valley," says Bagshaw in his *Kent*, "from the source of the Bourne upwards, is dry except after great rains and thaws of snow, when the springs of

The Little Stour

E

the Nailbourne overflow at Eltham and Lyminge, directing their course north-eastward, and then, by Barcham Downs northwards, descend into the head of the Bourne and blend their waters with it." The Little Stour is, like the Stour, an excellent chalk stream, and contains plenty of trout, which may average about three-quarters of a pound, though a good many run over the pound. Beaksbourne, on the London, Chatham, and Dover Railway, is a good centre for this pretty stream. The following flies are recommended:—yellow dun (good), pale evening dun, olive and red quills, alder, and Wickham. There is no May-fly season on the Little Stour. Ten brace of sizeable trout is not regarded as an exceptionally big bag.

The Darenth, or Darent as it was formerly called, **The Darenth** is the most troutful stream in the country. Spenser alluded to it thus :—

" . . . . . the still Darent, in whose waters clear
Ten thousand fishes play and deck his pleasant stream."

It is, too, one of the most charming of our lesser chalk streams in regard to scenery. The land through which it flows has been written of as the most beautiful of the Kentish vales ; and those who have wandered among the hop gardens and cherry orchards of Eynsford and noted the beauties of Darenth Wood will scarcely be disposed to cavil at this description. On its banks are many delightful seats, old manor houses, bits of an Elizabethan world like Franks near Farningham, and stately English houses like Lullingstone Castle. The Darenth, which was once famous for its salmon, rises near Westerham, and in its course of about thirty-three miles passes Sevenoaks, where Lord

Stanhope preserves, Otford, Shoreham, Eynesford,
Lullingstone Castle (Sir William Hart-Dyke's
water), Farningham, Horton Kirby and Dartford,
above which town there is an association of owners
of angling. A few sea trout, it is believed, are
still to be found from time to time at Dartford
Creek, and the river trout will, despite pollution,
occasionally venture below the town. Some years
ago the powder mills by polluting the water
destroyed thousands of trout; and a lawsuit which
went against the lessees of the mills, was the result.
Now once more there is a fair stock of good fish
a little above the town of Dartford. There are
several angling clubs on the Darenth, notably one
at Horton Kirby a little below the pretty town of
Farningham, and, owing to the nearness of London,
rods do not often go begging for long. Big bags
of trout have been often made by Darenth anglers.
I have before me particulars of one, perhaps the
record for the stream, of twenty-five brace of trout,
weighing just over fifty pounds. They were taken
on a stormy day towards the end of April. I have
also seen one or two large bags made in the
Lullingstone Castle water. The average size of
trout killed in Darenth is represented to me as
three-quarters of a pound, but from my own
experience and observation I should say that it is
somewhat smaller than this. In some parts of the
stream fish are very plentiful, and there the average
would be something under three-quarters of a
pound. Still deep pools, muddy bottoms, alternating
with streamy runs over gravel—such is the general
character of the stream. Here and there the banks
are well lined with willows and overgrown with a
tangle of vegetation, so that casting is far from

easy ; but on the whole the fishing is not rendered
very difficult through such obstacles, and wading
is scarcely ever necessary or excusable. The free
flow of the stream is much interfered with almost
every day during the best part of the angling
season by the action of mills, and sometimes the
fisherman has to wait hours for the water in the
height of the May-fly season. I have noticed that
when the water after being held up an hour or two
begins to flow once more in something like its
proper volume, trout frequently rise well for a short
period ; and this is the case on the Hertfordshire
Lea above Hatfield and various other streams.

At Eynsford there is a little trout water which
may be fished by those who purchase a daily ticket
at the Plough Inn, and the famous old hostelry the
Lion at Farningham has a short stretch above
Franks. There are sometimes plenty of fish in the
Lion water, and many a fighting three-quarter of a
pound trout has the writer had with dry fly out of
this pleasant stretch ; but these fish are anything
save easy to entice. A pound and a half trout is here
a decidedly good one, though from the bit of rapid
water to be fished from the pretty lawn of the old
inn, bigger fish have occasionally been taken. The
May-fly, as a rule, comes on in fair quantities on
the Darenth, though I cannot say I have myself
seen a very great hatch of the fly on this stream.
Some Darenth anglers still fish with the wet fly, while
others consider the wet fly most killing in April and
early May, and after that the dry fly. Personally
I have never succeeded in killing a sizeable trout
with anything but the dry fly on the Darenth, and
I consider the stream well adapted to this method.
Of course when the fish are very numerous and

little assailed the sunk fly may be relied upon to kill
in the early part of the season in most streams. I
have found no fly better than the olive dun or
olive quill on the Darenth with a sedge towards
night. An experienced Darenth angler gives the
following list of artificial flies for this stream :—
blue, olive, and yellow duns, olive quill, red quill,
governor, Wickham's fancy, May-fly with wings of
summer duck, coachman, cowdung, alder and sedge.
I have noticed the following natural flies on the
water: May-fly, olive or blue dun, yellow dun,
little may dun, Welshman's button and sedge.

The Cray must once have been a fine trout
stream, and even to-day it retains some vestiges of
its former greatness. It has been a good   The
deal polluted, however, and its volume of   Cray
water has sadly deteriorated, so that I hesitated
before giving it a place in the list of South Country
trout streams. The Cray rises at Orpington, and
runs a nine-mile course through the several Crays,
Bexley, and Crayford to the Darenth, which it joins
a mile below Dartford. The flow of water at Orpington used to be so considerable as to sometimes
flood the village, but the springs have now been not
a little reduced or lowered. There are still trout in
the stream at Bexley and at Messrs. Joynson's large
paper mills; but the fish, at the latter place, are
scarcely the genuine old Cray trout, which had red
flesh and were reputed to be very excellent for the
table. Mr. Joynson has kindly given me some information respecting the Cray and its trout, which
I cannot do better than quote in his own words.
"Some years ago," he writes, "before the Kent
Waterworks sunk their wells at Orpington, the
river Cray had plenty of water and some excellent

trout. That the trout were destroyed by the paper mills is not altogether true, although there have been times in the past when a pipe would burst in the winter and some strong chemicals go down the stream killing the fish. This has happened twice within my memory. Again, there have been times when people have intentionally put chloride of lime in the stream, killing thereby numbers of fish, which have been sold in the public houses for trifling sums. The finest fish we used to catch in the late Mr. Joynson's time—which is speaking of twenty-two years ago or more—were taken at the mill tail, where the water used for paper-making purposes used to run out into the river. Of late years we have used the sewer for the greater part of our water, more especially for such as would be polluted by the chemicals ; and it has been during that time principally that less and less fish have been seen in the stream. I have about a quarter of a mile of water above the mill where I keep some trout, most of which I have bought from various fisheries. I have tried several seasons to rear them myself, but only once with any success, for when they have reached the age of a few months from some cause or other they have all died." Mr. Joynson does not think that re-stocking the Cray would prove successful ; and he says, " I wonder where those trout which I put in the stream have gone to. They have somehow all disappeared, excepting the few which cannot get away unless there is a flooding ; then they go down the side cuttings and are not seen again."

The angling outlook therefore does not appear to be a rosy one, although it is certain that the fish which have been put in the stream and which have

stayed there have grown sometimes to a considerable size. Three- and even five-pounders have been
scaled during the spawning season.   The Cray is a
narrow stream, clear in some parts and rather thick
in others, and its pace is moderate.   Mr. Joynson
thinks that the anglers who once fished it used
gentles and other baits of the kind.   But a friend
tells me that in days long past he has had sport
with the artificial fly.   The Cray scarcely deserves
the name of chalk stream in the way that the Test
and Itchen do, though it flows through a country
the subsoil of which is here and there composed of
chalk as well as of loam, or heavy loam, or gravel.

CHAPTER II

THE SURREY, MIDDLESEX, AND SUSSEX STREAMS

THESE three counties may be grouped together, their trouting streams being somewhat few and far between. Middlesex has the Colne; Surrey the Wandle, the Tillingbourne, the Mole, and the Wey; whilst in Sussex there is the Rother, with several tributaries containing trout. There are other waters of course which contain trout, and I have myself taken some in the Western Rother, which does not, however, really merit even in its upper reaches the title of trout stream, any more than does the Arun, another of the coarse fish rivers of Sussex.

The Wandle is one of the most celebrated trout streams in England. "In Case-Haulton," wrote
The Wandle Thomas Fuller, "there be excellent trouts; so are there plenty of the best wallnuts, as if nature had observed the rule of physic, *Post pisces, nuces.*" Many writers have dwelt on the beauties of the stream and the country round about Carshalton. Davy described the Wandle as the "best and clearest stream near London"; and of the then village but now semi-suburban town, Walpole wrote that it was "as rural a village as if in

Northumberland, much watered with clearest streams, and buried in ancient trees of Scawen's Park and the neighbouring Beddington." Beddington, of whose "brave old hall" the same writer was enamoured, is now, alas, threatened grievously ; and Carshalton itself has, it would be idle to deny, in some respects suffered much since Ruskin, in a glowing passage in his *Crown of Wild Olive*, wrote thus :—" Twenty years ago there was no lovelier piece of lowland scenery in South England, nor any more pathetic in the world, by its expression of sweet human character and life, than that immediately bordering on the sources of the Wandle, and including the low moors of Addington, and the villages of Beddington and Carshalton, with all their pools and streams. No clearer or diviner waters ever sang with constant lips of the Hand which giveth rain from heaven ; no pastures ever lightened in spring-time with more passionate blossoming ; no sweeter homes ever hallowed the heart of the passer-by with their pride of peaceful gladness,—fain-hidden, yet full confessed." Thus Ruskin a quarter of a century ago : and Carshalton has its beauties still, but ugly City lamp-posts and modern flashy shop windows have made their mark on the place. It is inevitable perhaps with London "as a lion creeping nigher" every year, every month, almost, it might be said, every week ; but it is scarcely the less saddening for that. Then, as regards the stream, the mills have worked havoc— mills that grind slowly but grind exceeding small !

The banks of this chalkiest of chalk streams are often redolent in late summer with the aromatic odours of peppermint and sweet lavender, which are here cultivated in considerable quantities, and they

are full too of interesting historical memories.   It
was at Merton that our greatest of sea heroes and
deliverers used in intervals of peace to follow his
favourite pursuit of fly fishing ; and in Beddington
Park, where Queen Elizabeth once stayed a short
time, Sir Francis Carew first planted oranges from
pips brought across the Atlantic by another national
hero, Sir Walter Raleigh.   Beddington is not the
place for any but building experiments in these
times.   As for the poor Wandle at Merton, it is
a shocking sight and colour ; you might indeed as
well fly fish at Wandsworth as at Merton to-day.
Still there are two or three miles of the Wandle
yet left to the privileged angler, and in this short
length there are plenty of good trout to be hooked
now and then by the very skilful hand.   In
Carshalton itself there is a sheet of water where you
may often see a few fish cruising about, and both
above and below re-stocking has been persevered in.
The Wandle is here swelled by several clear and
copious springs.

The stream rises by Croydon and flows to
Beddington, Hackbridge, Carshalton, Mitcham,
and Merton.   It joins the Thames four and a
half miles down from the last named place, and
of course need not be considered as a trout
stream after it has left Mitcham.   The May-fly is
unknown on this water, and seems never to have
been a Wandle insect.   We find Davy remarking
on its absence early in the century.   The best
artificials are the small chalk stream patterns of
duns and quills ; and the best method of angling
is, I can hardly doubt, the dry fly.

The chief stretches are now in the hands of Mr.
J. H. Bridges (Lord of the Manor of Beddington) ;

Mr. Brown, who has lately stocked the stream at Waddon with both trout fry and roach; Mr. Dingwall; Mr. Frost; Mr. Brougham. Below the spot where the effluent of the Croydon sewage farm comes in Mr. Roberts, Mr. Easton (who has a small association), Mr. Deeds, the Wandle Fishing Association (which has a hatchery), and Mr. Bidder have most of the water. The Rev. T. Bentham is at the time of writing forming an angling club at Beddington Park, with a nine-inch limit for the first year and a ten-inch afterwards. The season is to be from May 1st to September 30th, and not more than three brace are to be taken by one rod in the day. Wandle trout run up to a good size. One of over 5 lbs was taken in Mr. Dingwall's water some years ago, which is the largest I have heard of.

Before leaving the Wandle I must refer to the way in which the stream has been polluted of late years. In order not to give unnecessary offence I have abstained, whilst quoting Ruskin, from giving the burning words of scorn which, in the preface to the *Crown of Wild Olive*, he pours upon those who desecrate our pure and lovely trout streams. Yet I feel that it would be wrong to altogether slur over the conduct of those who let loose the sewage of the town of Croydon into the Wandle, and let it loose in a state that cannot be far short of poisonous. If such pollution does not come under the Public Health Act of 1875, or the River Pollution Act of 1876, it is surely time for Parliament to further strengthen and extend the law in this matter.[1] The pestilential pollution of our living waters is a standing

[1] I hope the Thames Conservancy will try to purify the Wandle; it is their duty to do so.

reproach to civilisation. If we are so much more advanced in the science of drainage than our ancestors of a hundred years or so ago, how opaque must have been the darkness in which they dwelt in regard to these matters !

The Wey below Guildford never seems to have been regarded as a trout stream. Best had nothing

The Wey   to say of its trout at a time when he was ready to extol those of the Mole ; and in these days only an occasional fish is taken below Guildford. The Angling Society of that town, which numbers over a hundred members, has extensive fishing rights, and has done something towards getting up a small head of trout ; but we have to go above Godalming to get into the real trout-fishing portions of the stream. The Wey rises in Hampshire, one branch near Alton and the other near Selborne. The former, flowing by Farnham and Crooksbury Common, joins the latter —which passes Kingsley and Frensham—by Tilford, and the stream then flows by Elstead and through Pepperharrow park to Godalming. Both branches of the stream above Tilford are swelled by several little tributaries, some of which contain trout. There is for instance a small stream which comes from the beautiful Alice Holt wood, and joins the Alton branch a mile or two below Farnham ; whilst a stream coming from Ripley pond and another from Woolmer join the same branch further down. The Selborne branch receives several tributaries, amongst them a considerable one coming from near Haslemere, some of the springs of which supply the Crichmere fish ponds with very fine water. Trout are fairly plentiful in this branch, and of a good quality. In the upper

THE WEY, NEAR BENTLEY.

reaches they run decidedly small, but at Frensham
and Elstead two and three pounders may be taken.
Mr. Combe, of Pierpoint, has devoted a good deal of
trouble to the trouting in the Wey. He has had
many pike netted between Frensham and Elstead,
and the fishing in this part of the stream has much
improved, despite the presence of the otter. As
regards the Alton branch, there are but few trout
below Farnham. Above that town there are a
fair number of trout, if they do not run very large.
The whole of this branch is preserved, but the
otter has worked havoc in the lower stretches.
The May-fly comes on in large quantities, and the
alder and the willow fly are abundant. A fly called
Mellersh's fancy is recommended by some local
anglers for the Wey. " The stream," a Godalming
angler writes to me, " contains in parts many perch,
and some chub, pike, dace, and eels. It flows for the
most part through water meadows, and there are
very pretty little streams and pools in the upper
stretches ; but from Godalming downward it is
sluggish and uninteresting from a trout angler's
point of view."

The Mole has been a theme for not a few well-
known English authors, and the beauty of some of
its scenery in the neighbourhood of The
Dorking, Bletchworth, and Mickleham— Mole
once described by Sir James Mackintosh as "the
happy valley "—is undeniable. From Leatherhead
to Stoke d'Abernon, too, the stream is very pretty,
flowing, as one of its most ardent admirers has
pleasantly expressed it,—

> " Through quiet meadows, rich
>   In yellow cowslips and the tall foxglove
>   With its deep purple bells."

The Mole rises near Crawley in Sussex and runs
to Horley, two miles and a half below which place
a stream coming from Rowfant joins. Afterwards
it passes Bletchworth, Dorking, Box Hill, Leatherhead, Cobham, Esher, and Moulsey, below which it
unites with the Thames. The Mole is a somewhat
turbid stream, yet it seems to have always held
good trout long before any one thought of stocking
it with fry or yearlings, which has been done in
several stretches. Of old it was noted for its excellent fish. Best, in his account of the principal
rivers in England, speaking of it as being "stored
with plenty of good trout, fat and large." In Best's
time there were trout so far down as Esher, where
there are certainly none to-day. To reach the
trouting portion of the stream the angler has to go
six or eight miles above that town to the neighbourhood of Leatherhead.

The upper waters of the Mole about Horley are
of small account. They contain no trout at the
present time, though there are a few fish in the
tributaries, and occasionally May fly are seen there
in small numbers. Just below Horley Mill the
Horley sewage farm discharges its resultant waters
into the stream, and this seems to have spoilt the
fishing for several miles down. It is amazing that
in these days our streams should be so often
turned into more or less open sewers. It is well
known that several of the most dreaded of diseases
invariably travel down stream, and surely no better
way of giving them a chance of spreading could be
devised than the practice of letting our "living
waters" carry down sewage and the like.

The Mole is celebrated for what are called its
Swallow Holes at various spots between Box Hill

and Leatherhead. These swallows are said by some to be gullies leading to fissures in the chalk rock beneath, not absorbing the water but receiving and draining it off in subterranean channels ; yet on the other hand, says Lewis in his *Book of English Rivers*, there is no positive evidence that the waters thus engulfed are the same as those which spring forth towards Leatherhead. The Mole, as I have mentioned elsewhere, is by no means the only English stream which goes underground at certain points. The Deverell in Wiltshire is noted for the same peculiarity, as are one or two streams in the North of England. The Mole is a favourite stream with various water birds. At Fetcham the coot has established itself, and the kingfisher is constantly to be seen about and above Leatherhead. The latter bird is by no means so scarce on our southern streams as some suppose, and last year I was delighted to find it in something like plenty on several waters in the home counties.

The Tillingbourne was unhappily poisoned a good many years ago, and quite robbed of its trout, but it has been re-stocked, and is now one of the best and most agreeable of the Surrey angling streams. It is some eight or nine miles long, and rises in Abinger Common. During its course to the Wey, which it joins at Shalford, the Tillingbourne passes Gomshall and Shere, where it feeds some lakes in Albury Park. The Tillingbourne is easily affected by rain, and soon gets muddy. After being thoroughly discoloured it takes the best part of two days to clear. Its pace is rather slow, and besides trout it contains a few pike, perch, dace, roach, together with gudgeon. The trout killed averag about 1 lb., but they run up to 2 lbs. and occasionally 3 lbs. There is a rise of May-fly, and the favourite artificials are olive duns, red spinners, and March browns. The style of fly fishing is either wet or dry. Colonel Godwin-Austen preserves the Tillingbourne as high as Chilworth, and his water has been re-stocked at various times. The late Mr. Andrews put some yearlings into the stream after it had been poisoned years ago, and the experiment proved very successful. The angler may stay at either Shalford or Gomshall, both of which places are on the South Eastern Railway.

The Colne is a somewhat poor looking stream above its junction with the much more attrac-

The Colne. tive Ver. It rises not far from Hatfield and meets the Ver two miles or so below Park Street. Thence, swelled by a brook from Elstree, the Colne runs to Watford ; Rickmansworth, where it receives the Gade and Chess (which are dealt with in the chapters on Hertfordshire and Buckinghamshire); Harefield; Denham; Uxbridge; and West Drayton. Below West Drayton there are no trout ; and the Colne, passing Colnbrook, joins the Thames a mile from Wraysbury. The Colne, I am sorry to say, has, like the Wandle and Mole, suffered much of late years from sewage pollution ; but the prospects of the angler now that the Thames Conservancy is actively moving in the matter, are really beginning to look a little brighter. The Colne from Rickmansworth to West Drayton has several very pretty and celebrated places on or near its banks. There is Moor Park, referred to elsewhere, and Denham Court, where Dryden wrote his First Georgic, and where Charles II. is supposed to have once lain concealed. "Nature has conspired with art to make the garden one of the most delicious spots in England," wrote the poet with enthusiasm of Denham Court. Then, too, there is Denham Place, with its pretty fishery. This is the scene of Sir Humphry Davy's angling meet between Halieus, Poietes, Ornither, and Phyxius. In the days of Sir Humphry the Colne was a pure trout stream, and there was a rule at Denham against killing a trout in the May-fly season of under 2 lbs. —a rule, by the way, that made Poietes declare with some testiness, " I cannot say that I approve of this manner of fishing ; I lose all my labour." Denham has been famous for its fine trout in much more recent times than Sir Humphry Davy's ; but the fishing seems to have begun to deteriorate while the late General Goodlake was living there. He stocked the Colne so far back as 1874 with American brook trout,—an experiment, like others of the same kind, not attended with success.

The Colne, dividing Middlesex from Buckingham, runs in several branches to Uxbridge and West Drayton, where it receives a tributary coming from Ruislip reservoir. There is some free water on Uxbridge Moor, where a certain number of trout are taken by various methods—not many, I am afraid, with the fly ; and at West Drayton there is the well-known angling club bearing that name, with its club house at Thorney Weir. The trout fishing begins on the club water on April 1st and ends on September 30th. Re-stocking has been tried, not altogether without some little success ; but the Colne here is too full of coarse fish to be a really good trout water, and fly fishing does not yield good baskets. A large fly fished down

F

stream is more likely to prove successful than small
duns and spinners fished dry, and out of May-fly
season, indeed, I gather that wet fly fishing is the
most effective on most parts of the Colne. I can
find no record of the trout of the Colne, which are
usually large and few and far between, taking any
imitation of the natural fly well out of the drake
season. "The true season for the Colne," said Davy
—who, as we gather from the *Last Days of a Philosopher*, often used to fish in the stream—"is the
season of the May-fly." The Alexandra, a somewhat obnoxious, and by some held to be scarcely a
legitimate, lure, is, I believe, occasionally used by
Colne, as well as Thames, anglers. On delicate
waters, where the trout rise properly at small fly,
its use may well be prohibited by clubs and proprietors of fishing. It seems to often scratch far
more fish than it actually hooks. I admit I have
used it myself on the Colne near Harefield at my
angling host's own suggestion, though not with
much pleasure or success.

There is a marked dearth of fly on the Colne
at and about West Drayton, which Mr. Murray,
the proprietor of the water, attributes, rightly or
wrongly, to the sewage pollution and "the early
machine cutting of grass." Whether the sewage
kills the fly or not, it is certain that it kills fly
fishing ; and I have in my mind several cases
where it is impossible in hot weather to approach
certain parts of more than one trout stream,
owing to the disgusting odour. The attempt to
prove that sewage pollution is rather good than
otherwise for the trout cannot be put forward
seriously by any one with the least knowledge of
fish and fish life. The few big black trout which

frequent the polluted points of streams are a disgrace to their species.

The Rother might, small doubt, be greatly improved as a trout stream above Bodiam, where it is naturally a clear and clean stream **The** and fairly rapid in pace ; but at present it **Rother** contains too many coarse fish to allow of its being a really good trout water. It has, however, several tributaries, such as the Tillingham and the Brede, which contain plenty of small trout. The Rother itself is preserved by the Rother Fishing Association. The trout fishing season commences on April 1st and ends on September 1st, and no trout of under half a pound can be taken. Trout of over 1 lb are not often killed, though fish have been taken up to 2½ lbs and 3½ lbs. The May-fly and the olive duns are the chief flies, but as a matter of fact fly fishing is rarely attempted. The Rother flows by Ticehurst, Etchingham, and Robertsbridge, and enters the sea at Rye. Its tributaries, the Brede and Tillingham, are private. It contains some heavy pike, and abundance of bream, chub, and dace. In the moat at Bodiam Castle, a fine place well worthy of a visit, there are said to be some heavy perch. Below Bodiam trout fishing is out of the question. The Rother Fishery District includes all streams between Fairlight and Dungeness.

CHAPTER III

THE HERTFORDSHIRE STREAMS

THE Hertfordshire streams, though not by any means so famous as those of Hampshire or so numerous as those of Devon, demand a chapter to themselves. Hertfordshire is watered by, first, the Lea with its tributaries the Mimram or Maran ; the Beane ; the Rib with its tributary the Quin ; and the Ash : secondly, by the Colne with its tributaries the Ver or Verlam ; the Gade with its tributary the Bulbourne ; and for a few miles the Buckinghamshire Chess : and, thirdly, in the extreme northern corner of the county, by a mile or two of the Ivel and the Ivel's tributary the Hiz. All these streams are trout-bearing. The Stort, a tributary of the Lea dividing the county from Essex, is essentially a coarse fish water. The Rhee, also, which flows for a few miles through the northern corner of the county to join the Cam in Cambridgeshire shortly after passing the border, is a coarse fish stream. In the extreme east of the county the Thame has one of its head waters, but this is not a trout stream.

The Lea between Hertford and its source, which is six miles north-west of Luton in Bedfordshire has some of the best trouting in England. **The** At various places between Luton Park **Lea** lake and Hatfield Park the trout run very big, and in the club water above Hatfield in particular there is a backstream famous for its four and five pound-fish; nor is a four pound trout by any means an extraordinarily heavy fish for the river at Brocket or at Wheathampstead. The old Lea trout is believed by some to be a distinct variety, but re-stocking has introduced various other strains such as Loch Levens, and also trout from the Wick and the Test. The Lea is a chalk stream, fairly clean and pure in its upper lengths or head waters, containing large quantities of the fresh-water shrimp, on which trout always thrive so well. Grayling have been introduced, but—fortunately perhaps—do not seem to have taken very kindly to the water. There are a few big ones in Hatfield Park, and so high up as Wheathampstead I have myself taken one with a May-fly. They rarely rise, however, at an artificial fly. Coarse fish, particularly pike and dace, are still too plentiful in many lengths, and here and there in the deeper holes there are some fair perch. The cream of the trout fishing on this stream is in the May-fly season, and the insect often comes in great quantities on most lengths from Luton to Hatfield. Some of the heavy fish frequenting the more sluggish water then rise for a week or so at the artificial fly, but can rarely be induced to look at it at any other season. The natural flies fre-quenting the Lea include, besides the May-fly, the olive or blue dun, the yellow dun, the little May dun (in small quantities), the turkey brown, and the alder. For dry fly fishing, which is the most telling method when the water is fine and the weather fair, the ordinary chalk stream patterns of duns, Wickhams, red quills, red spinners, and Mayflies, together with the alder—a capital fly for this river—the March brown—which may possibly be taken for the turkey brown by the trout—and the governor. In boisterous weather when the dry fly is impracticable, or when no fish are rising, a large sunk alder, used in the way described in Chapter I, is often very effective. Below Hatfield the Lea flows through some pretty scenery, but in parts is inclined to be too deep and sluggish for a genuine trouting water. Below Hertford it is a coarse fish water, containing a few heavy trout. After leaving Broxbourne it speedily begins to lose its rural aspect. The Crown Inn at that place has long been famous among anglers, and it boasts what has been described as "the finest example of flower gardening in the kingdom." Luton, Wheathampstead, Hatfield, and Hertford, are good headquarters for the Lea trout fisherman. Hertford is within easy reach, not only of the lower trouting waters of the Lea, but also of those of several of the Lea's tributaries, such as the Beane, the Rib, and the Mimram,

The Mimram is the best of the several tributaries of the Lea. This dainty little chalk stream rises

The Mimram about five miles north-west of Codicote, and, after forming a lake at Kimpton Hoo, Lord Hampden's place, runs through the very pretty village of Welwyn, where Young, author of the *Night Thoughts*, was once pastor, through Tewin and through Panshanger to the Lea at Hertford. At no

point is its scenery anything save charming ; and at
Panshanger, Lord Cowper's seat, the oaks are
worth a day's journey to see. In the park there is
one tree surpassing perhaps anything in Brocket,
and as celebrated as Queen Elizabeth's tree in
Hatfield. It is called the Panshanger oak, and
has been described by Strutt, Loudon, and other
leading writers on forestry. The whole of the
Mimram is strictly preserved through its course of
fourteen miles or so. Above Welwyn the average
weight of the trout killed is about a pound, but at
several points below the fish run considerably
heavier than this. The trouting in Tewin and
Panshanger Park is particularly good. In the
upper parts of the stream the trout rise well at the
artificial fly throughout the season, provided there
is sufficient water. There is a May-fly season,
which usually commences at the end of May, but
the insect is never so numerous on the Mimram
as on the Lea. There are fair hatches of olive
or blue duns, and occasionally of yellow duns ;
and the chalk stream patterns may be used for
dry fly fishing. In the lower reaches of the
Mimram the trout do not rise so freely at the
small fly as they do higher up. The stream,
like the Lea, is essentially a " fat " one, full of water
shrimps and other similar food on which trout thrive
greatly. High up towards Codicote, where the
stream is small and comparatively rapid, there is
rarely anything in the nature of a late evening rise,
but lower down, on the other hand, the late evening
is commonly the best time in the summer. The
Mimram is a clear and pure stream. The angler
finds his headquarters at Hertford or Welwyn.
At the latter there is a capital inn, the Wellington

Arms. The surrounding country is pretty and well wooded—good for cycling, driving, or walking.

The Beane, or Beame, is also a good trout stream. It rises near Stevenage, on the Great **The** Northern Railway, near the borders of **Beane** Cambridgeshire, and flows due south to the Lea at Hertford. In the upper parts of the stream trout are by no means plentiful, but what there are run large. I have before me a record of eight trout averaging 3½lbs., taken by an angler last summer in the upper Beane. The May-fly comes on in considerable quantities, but small fly is not very effective. An alder is a good fly, but a more gaudy fly, such as the Alexandra, is deemed by some anglers the best of all. Re-stocking has been resorted to by several proprietors of fishing, but hundreds of trout have been destroyed by severe droughts, and above Walkern the fish are consequently far from being too numerous. The best water on the Beane is perhaps at Frogmore, the estate of Mr. Hudson, M.P. Here there are plenty of trout, and the water is carefully preserved and looked after. The fishing on the Beane is in private hands, and there are no angling clubs, as there are on the Lea and Mimram. High banks in places and a gravelly bed are characteristics of the stream. At Woodhall Park the stream expands into a lake, in which there are some large fish, and five miles on it joins the Lea. Watton, or Walkern may be made headquarters by the angler.

The Rib also flows into the Lea just below Hertford. It rises a few miles from Buntingford and after a course of some eight miles is joined by the Quin. It then flows to the Lea in a south-easterly

direction, passing How Street station, Standon,
and Thundridge. This stream, like the Quin,
flows through a quiet country half arable
and half pasture. It is a chalk stream **The Rib**
with a bed now of mud and now of gravel. In some
parts of the stream trout are plentiful, but not near
the Lea, where coarse fish are too abundant. In
the upper parts of the Rib a sizable trout is one of
three quarters of a pound. Fish run to 3lbs., and I
have a record of one weighing 5½lbs. Lower down
stream the weight of trout killed varies from 1lb.
to 2lbs. The May-fly comes on about May 20th,
and lasts a fortnight or so. This, the alder and
Wickham fancy are good flies for the lower portion of the stream, and the dry fly method of
angling when the stream is fairly clear seems to
be the most effective. The Rib is a sluggish
water, seldom very bright and after heavy rain
it becomes decidedly foul, and at such times
the dry fly is not of course of much good. A
gentleman who has fished the upper portions of
the stream for a quarter of a century recommends
the following flies :—March brown, May fly, alder,
coachman, red and black palmers, coch-a-bonddu
and the ordinary duns. He says that the fish
have grown far more wary than when he first
angled for them, and he no longer gets the large
baskets he once did in May fly time. A great deal
of re-stocking at various times has taken place, and
there are now two angling clubs on the stream, one
at Standon and the other—just starting—at
Youngsbury. The coarse fish of the Rib include
pike, perch, dace, roach, chub, and gudgeon. These
thrive principally in the lower portions of the stream,
which is much overgrown and very weedy.

The Quin is received by the Rib at Hammels
Park.   It runs a ten-mile course, rising in the
The north-east corner of the county, and flow-
Quin ing in a south-east direction through Great
and Little Hormead.   The Quin resembles the
Rib in regard to the character of the country it
passes through.   It has fewer coarse fish than the
Rib, and the average weight of its trout is perhaps
a little below that of the larger stream.   The fish
do not often turn the scale at 1½ lbs., and they are
less numerous than they were.   There are no angling
clubs on this little stream, and it is difficult—as it is
in the case of the Rib—to obtain leave.   Braughing
is a centre for the trout angler who has leave on
either stream or on both.   The May fly comes
on at the same time as on the Rib, and the
same flies do for both streams.   Above Braughing
the Quin, like various other streams, goes underground in dry weather, and sometimes fish going
up in a flood get stranded.   I am afraid at Hormead a rake is deemed under these circumstances
the best angling implement !   The head waters of
the Lea, the upper Mimram and the Beane, all
suffer severely from droughts from time to time,
and it is found necessary to make small wooden
dams to hold up the water.   Last year (1897)
there was, however, abundance of water in most of
our south country trout streams—more than enough
to last the entire angling season.

The Ash or Ashe is the last tributary of the Lea
with which it is necessary to deal.   This stream,
The Ash which is just about the length of the Quin,
rises at Furneaux Pelham and, flowing
through Hadham Cross and Widford, joins the
Lea at St. Margarets.   The upper part of the

stream has deteriorated. Years ago it yielded
some good trout, weighing from one to three
pounds, but now there are only a few smaller ones
to be taken. Below Murdock's mill to the junction
with the Lea, the water is carefully preserved and
stocked by Mr. Fowell Buxton. The May-fly
season is the best time for taking trout in the Ash,
but the artificials recommended for the Rib or
Quin hold good for this stream also. The Ash
flows through a nice country—" pleasant Hertfordshire," as Charles Lamb called it. There are no
angling clubs on the stream, but the water is let by
the property owners on both banks. The trout
fisherman will perhaps find the best quarters at
Ware ; though, for the matter of that, there should
be room for him at Widford, a village which
rejoices in five public houses divided among a
population of 453 all told !

The Ivel. Very little of this stream actually belongs to Hertfordshire. The stream rises near
Baldock, in the extreme north of the The Ivel
county, and joins the Ouse about midway
between Bedfordshire and St. Neots. It runs
through a flat and not very interesting country,
save for a few miles about Shefford, where there
are some pretty hills and woods. Ivel trout are
particularly fine, owing to some extent, no doubt,
to the abundance of fresh water shrimp which
the stream produces. They are grey spotted with
greyish brown, and they cut very pink. Cen-
turies ago the Ivel was stocked by means of spawn
brought from the now extinct fish ponds of St.
Albans Abbey, which ponds, in their turn, were
supplied with trout brought from the Abbey water
of a place in Normandy. At present the trout are

not exactly plentiful, but there are a fair number running from 1½ lbs. up to as much as 5 lbs. Very few fish of under the former weight are to be seen, but sometimes much larger ones are taken. At Astwick Mill a 13-lb. trout, I believe, has been killed, and in the mill head at Radwell, in Hertfordshire, an 8-lb. trout was captured only last summer (1897). There is no May-fly, and the favourite artificials are the Wickham, the blue or olive dun, and the governor. The trout are anything but free risers at the fly. There are no clubs on the Ivel.

The Hiz, or Hir, is a tributary of the Ivel, which it joins at Arlesby, in Bedfordshire. It rises at **The Hiz** Hitchen, a pleasant town in north Hertfordshire, and one of the few places in this country where lavender and peppermint are successfully cultivated. Here it has three branches, is a capital trout stream, and is well stocked and looked after. Both the Hiz and the Ivel have been stocked by Mr. Christian, who resides at the Norton Mills at Radwell, and takes much interest in pisciculture. Some of the trout put in these North Hertfordshire waters came from the lower Mimram, near Panshanger, where there are some splendid fish. The Hiz is, unfortunately, subjected, as is the Ivel, to a good deal of sewage, and as a result many fish turned black and perished last season. The Hiz is a May-fly stream, and the trout run large, as in the Ivel.

The Rhee, a tributary of the Cam, rising in North Hertfordshire, is not a trout stream. We may therefore turn south again and consider the Ver and the Gade. The Colne, which is unworthy of much notice until it is joined by the Ver near Park Street, is dealt with as a Middlesex stream, and the lower lengths of the Chess which flow through the south-east of the county are not of much note.

The Ver, or Verlam, rises north of Redbourne— according to the ordnance map, almost as high as Markyat Street, in Bedfordshire. In its upper reaches it is not a very bright trout **The Ver** stream, and I have more than once noted a kind of curious and most objectionable scum constantly rising to the surface, and covering the fly and hook. It contains some good trout, though dace and other coarse fish are rather too plentiful, and restocking has been successfully carried on by several owners and renters of water. The evening is, as a rule, the best time for fly fishing, but the trout do not often rise in the upper parts very well to the natural fly. The small dry fly is not nearly so good, as a rule, as a large fancy artificial. I have never myself seen the May-fly on the river above St. Albans, though I have heard of it there. About the mills some very heavy trout may occasionally be seen in the summer evenings, and the average weight of the fish killed will scarcely be under $1\frac{1}{2}$ lbs. Below St. Albans, and at Park Street, and near its junction with the Colne, the Ver is a much more taking looking trout stream, reminding one in parts of the genuine south country chalk stream.

The Gade is scarcely, from an angling point of view, one of the most attractive of the Hertford- shire trout streams. It is easily dis- **The** coloured, and is commonly regarded as **Gade** a somewhat "sick" looking water. The Gade, which is joined by a short tributary called the Bulbourne at Two Waters, rises between Little and Great Gaddesden, runs a fourteen-mile course by Hemel Hempstead, Boxmoor, and King's Langley, and flows into the Colne at Rickmansworth. On its banks, or near by, are two or three notable places, such as Grove Park, belonging to the Earl of Clarendon ; Cassiobury, belonging to the Earl of Essex, "a noble and delicious seat," as it has been called ; and Moor Park. Of the last named, Sir William Temple said, "It is the sweetest place I think that I have ever seen in my life at home or abroad."

Trout are pretty plentiful in the Gade, and they run up to 3 lbs.[1] The largest of which I have a reliable record was 5 lbs. The red spinner and the march brown are capital flies on this stream, and the May-fly comes on in the last week in May. There are no angling clubs on the Gade, which is nearly all strictly preserved by the riparian owners. The springs of the Gade are very numerous, and the stream flows between chalk hills with a clay soil.

[1] The Gade in Cassiobury Park contains more trout of large size than I ever saw in an English stream. In June 1897, the Hon. Sydney Holland landed upwards of eighty with the May-fly in a single day. The following day, fishing for a short time only, I landed thirty-one, keeping nine which weighed 13½ lbs.—ED.

CHAPTER IV

THE BUCKS, OXON, AND GLOUCESTERSHIRE STREAMS

ONLY portions of Oxfordshire and Gloucestershire can be regarded as situated in the south
country, and I propose, therefore, to deal with but
a few of the trout streams of these counties. Of
the seven trout streams considered in this chapter,
three, the Chess, the Misbourne, and the Wick,
belong to Buckinghamshire, and flow through
the south-east corner of the county; Oxford has
the lower parts of the Windrush, which flows
through the west of the county ; whilst the upper
Windrush, the Coln, and the Leach, running
almost parallel to one another in a south-east
direction, join the left bank of the Thames between Eynsham and Lechlade. Lastly there is
the Gloucestershire Frome—not to be confounded
with the Somersetshire Frome—which flows through
the western part of the county and joins the
(Bristol) Avon. Some of the streams of this
county, which formerly contained trout, are now
spoilt ; and among them the Little Avon must, I
am afraid, be included.

The Chess is in truth a lovely trout stream, flowing through one of the most charming and **The** fruitful districts in the home counties. **Chess** Rising close to Chesham, it flows past that town, then on to Latimer and Chenies, through a land of high chalk hills crowned with beeches, to join the Colne at Rickmansworth. Two more prosperous or two prettier villages than Latimer, which belongs to Lord Chesham, and Chenies, which is almost entirely owned by the Duke of Bedford, it would be very hard to find in the south of England. The position of Chenies, on a wooded hillside overlooking the little valley through which the Chess flows, is perfect. The village green, with its knot of "immemorial elms"; the large red-brick cottages, nearly all built on the same model, and yet far from conveying a sense of monotony; the trim little gardens, ablaze in the summer months with the old flowers the cottager all over our land loves; the ivy covered Tudor house, with oriel windows, where Queen Elizabeth once tarried on her way to Hatfield; and the church with its splendid Russell Chapel, all combine to make Chenies an ideal English village. Despite its fame and the fact that it is almost within the magnetic influence of London, Chenies has escaped the contamination of the city. No hideous street lamps have here been erected by enterprising local authorities, and no appalling hoardings, or the like, announce "This desirable plot of land to be let for building purposes." Carshalton has been taken, but Chenies, thanks to a great family, left.

The Chess is well stored with fine trout, which do not, however, often run to a very large size. Big baskets have been and still are made on this

stream, and Froude was scarcely guilty of an un-
pardonable exaggeration when he enthusiastically
declared, "a day's fishing at Chenies means a day
by the best water in England in the fisherman's
paradise of solitude." The May-fly is very variable
on the Chess, some seasons hatching only in small
quantities and at others in great profusion. In
1896 there was a very great hatch of the May-fly.
The olive dun is the chief insect on the Chess,
appearing throughout the season ; indeed, after the
end of the season of 1897 I noticed a really good
hatch of olives on a sunny autumnal afternoon,
and trout taking them freely. The artificial flies
commonly used by anglers are the March brown,
olive or blue dun, red spinner, alder, black gnat,
governor, and a large grey sedge. Besides trout
and grayling, the stream in parts contains perch,
roach, and pike. Some American brook trout
(*fontinalis*) and rainbow trout (*irideus*) were put
in the water some seasons since near Chesham.

Both wet and dry fly are used, but in the rougher
water the former seems to account for the better
baskets. On the other hand, there are pieces of
water on the stream, as, for instance, the still
stretch above the mill and fall at Chenies, which
are particularly well adapted to the floating fly
over the rising trout; and it is here that some of
the best trout are to be found. Sad to relate, this
beautiful trout stream has been badly polluted in
parts by sewage ; yet to look at, in its upper and
middle lengths, the Chess seems the finest of
waters.

The Misbourne runs through a small valley with
somewhat wooded low hills on either side, and it
extends from Great Missenden to Denham on the

G

Colne.   It waters some considerable lakes at Missenden Abbey and Shardloes, and then passes
The Mis- Amersham, a pleasant Buckinghamshire
bourne town, Chalfont St. Giles, and Chalfont St.
Peters.   The best trouting is in the five miles of
stream between the last named village and the
Colne, and this is well preserved.   The angler may
stay at the Bull at Gerrard's Cross, or at Denham.   Trout are pretty plentiful, running up to a
good size, and the May-fly comes on in fair
quantities.   Chalfont St. Giles, a pretty village, is
famous through its associations with Milton, who
lived here during the time when the Great Plague
was raging, correcting some of the sheets of
Paradise Lost and writing *Paradise Regained.*
Gurney's mill on this stream is said to be the
oldest in England.

The Wick, Wyk, or Wye, rises in a mill pool at
West Wycombe, and passing High Wycombe,
The Loudwater, and Woburn joins the Thames
Wick between Cookham and Bourne End
bridges.   The Wick is sadly polluted in its lower
lengths.   It is on the whole, however, a clear chalk
stream, working a number of mills.   Several of these
mills are for the manufacture of paper, and some
years ago the trout were decimated by them.
Latterly much greater care has been taken to avoid
poisoning the water, and as a result there has been
next to no injury done to the fish in the first six
miles or so of the stream.[1]

The Wick, or, as they are more commonly
called, the Wycombe trout, are celebrated, one
might almost say, the world over.   They are ex-

[1] Since writing this I see that a number of good fish have
been killed by a bad case of pollution.

ceptionally short thick fish with small heads ; they have very red flesh ; and they are spotted with black, and have silvery bellies. The trout of the Antipodes are not unlike those of the Wick either in form or in colour, and as a matter of fact, ova of Wycombe trout were sent out to New Zealand when the ultimately successful experiments in pisciculture were being made there : indeed the ova of Wick trout were included in the first consignment which safely reached its destination. Mr. William Senior, among others, has testified to the similarity between the New Zealand and the Wycombe trout, and the New Zealand anglers of the remote future may, perhaps, come to speak of St. Wycombe ! The Wycombe trout run large, averaging quite a pound, and being occasionally taken up to 4 lbs. and 5 lbs. in some parts of the stream. Mr. Thurlow with a large wet fly once captured in a single evening a trout of over 5 lbs. and another of over 7 lbs. in a stretch of water above High Wycombe, and both fish were exhibited for a while in Farlow's window in the Strand. There is no May-fly on the Wick, but alder, olive, yellow, and watery duns. The artificial flies most in demand are red, blue and grey quill gnats, olive duns and quills, red spinner, hare's car, alder, and black gnat. Dry fly fishing is usual, though the wet fly is found of service in the early part of the season.

The High Wycombe Angling and Trout Pre-servation Association has two miles of the Wick. Its season begins on May 1 and closes on September 30, and no member is allowed to fish more than two days in the week, or to kill more than two brace of fish in the day. One brace of trout of eleven inches or over may be taken, but the fish

of the second brace must not be less than twelve
inches each. Wading is not allowed, and the artificial fly is the only lure that can be used on the
Association water.

The Windrush, the upper part of which belongs
to Gloucestershire and the lower to Oxfordshire, is
The not one of the chalk streams. The "nitrous
Wind- Windrush," as it has been called, flows
rush through a country the subsoil of which
varies considerably; thus, for instance, we find
gravel at Bourton-on-the-Water, clay and brash
at Great Rissington, rock at Widford, and gravel
and rock at Burford. The stream rises at
Ginting Power in Gloucestershire. Seven miles
below this place is Bourton-on-the-Water, which
can be made headquarters by the angler who
desires to fish the upper Windrush or the Dickler,
a tributary of about six miles in length, containing trout, which rises at Donnington Mill
and joins the larger stream between Bourton
and Rissington. Trout in the Dickler run smaller
than in the Windrush, and the flies and method of
angling are common to both waters. After passing
Rissington, the Windrush receives an unimportant
tributary and flows by Windrush, Barrington,
Tainton, Burford, Witney, Ducklington, and Stan-
lake. It joins the left bank of the Thames seven
miles above Eynsham. In its upper portions the
Windrush may be described as a fairly clear stream
flowing at a medium pace; but below, at Burford
and Witney, it is usually inclined to be rather a
thick water, and at the former place its pace is on
the whole slow. At and about Bourton trout run
up to 2 lbs., and the wet fly would seem to be
the most usual way of taking them. In the May-

fly season, however, a floating fly is now often used. The March brown, I am told, appears on this water, but I have not seen it there myself. The artificial flies used include the March brown, blue uprights, alder, olive dun, yellow dun, red spinner, and May-fly. There are some grayling in the Windrush above Bourton, with chub and dace below the village. Down stream, at Burford and thereabouts, the trout run up to 5 lbs., and only rise at a May-fly or else at an Alexandra or some other large fly of a fancy pattern. The average weight of the trout killed need not be put at under 2 lbs., smaller fish being rarely taken. Pike, chub, roach, dace, and gudgeon are found in the water, and no re-stocking with trout has been resorted to nearer to Burford than Barrington. In the upper reaches of the Windrush there has been no re-stocking at all within the last half century. Some of the scenery on the Windrush is decidedly picturesque, and Bourton and Naunton are among the prettier villages on this stream.

The Coln has been gauged to be the fastest flowing trout stream in Gloucestershire. It is a beautifully clear water, and passes through **The Coln** a country the subsoil of which varies between stone brash, stone, freestone, and gravel. Rising by Shipton in a mill pond the Coln flows a distance of about twenty-seven miles to the Thames, with which it unites at Lechlade. Among the places the Coln passes are Wittington, Yanworth, the three Coln villages, Bibury, and Fairford, which is six miles from the Thames. Bibury or Fairford is a convenient resort for the angler who has not permission to fish private portions of the stream, there being excellent stretches of water at both these places which can be fished by ticket. The angler may stay at The Swan at Bibury or The Bull at Fairford. The proprietor of the Upper Coln Trout Fishery is Mr. Woodman of the former place. The Coln is an admirable stream for the dry fly angler, and at Bibury and Fairford as well as at the Colns it is unusual to find the angler fishing in any other way. The fish killed average perhaps a little over 1 lb., the usual limit being ¾ lb. or 11 inches. A few March browns are to be seen on the Coln, and there is a good rise of May-fly. The artificials used on this stream include the usual chalk stream patterns of quills and duns, together with the alder, sedge, Ogden's fancy, hawthorn, cowdung, black gnat, and governor. A pattern of the sherry spinner (the *imago* of the blue winged olive dun), tied by Mr. Lockwood of Bibury, is also well spoken of. The Coln has been re-stocked in parts, and the results have been satisfactory. There are but few coarse fish in the stream till near the Thames, where big dace and chub are found ; whilst crayfish, though diminished in quantity as in many other waters, are still noticed here and there.

The Leach, a stream of some 19 miles in length, rises at North Leach in Gloucestershire, and flows The by the villages of East Leach, Turville, Leach Southrop, and Little Faringdon. It joins the Thames a mile below Lechlade. The Leach is a clear stream, flowing through a country the subsoil of which is often rock, and it contains at the present time plenty of trout averaging about ¾ lb., though some are inclined to think that the head of fish is not so considerable as it used to be. There is often a good May-fly season, and then

fifteen to twenty brace forms by no means an exceptionally big basket for the stream. At other
seasons, when the trout are rising, a basket of five
or six is regarded as a pretty good one. Dry-fly
fishing is usually practised on the Leach, but when
the wind is adverse a wet fly is often used. The
best wind for this stream is an east or north-east
one, and then the dry fly proves, as a rule, most
killing; whilst south and south-west wind is bad for
fly fishing. The usual duns and quills may be used
by the dry fly angler. The alder is a very good fly
for dry and wet fly anglers alike, and it need not be
tied on too small a hook. There are no angling
clubs on the Leach, and the water is all in private
hands, the best parts belonging to Lord de Mauley.
Little Faringdon, the nearest railway station to
which is Lechlade, is about the best place for the
angler to stay at.

The Frome rises near Chipping Sodbury, and,
flowing by Yate, Frampton Cotterell, Iron Acton
and Stapleton Road Station, joins the   The
Avon at Bristol. The Frome is rapid, and   Frome
in fine weather the water is quite clear ; but it is
rather subject to floods after heavy rain, and then
soon gets discoloured. Shallows and deep stretches
alternate. In many places the Frome rushes over
a stony bed, whilst in others there are long pools
of five or six feet in depth. The stream has been
well stocked at Frampton by the Clifton Angling
Society, and trout are taken up to about 2½ lbs.
The May-fly hatches in considerable quantities,
and is taken well by the trout. Dry and wet fly
can both be used. In addition to trout, the Frome
contains, like its tributaries the Laden and Bradley,
roach, dace, perch, and gudgeon, and the coarse

fish angling is in various parts of the stream often decidedly good ; but poaching by nets and dyna-mite has been much too common of late years, and the Avon and Brue Fishery Board might with advantage lay itself out to put an end to this state of things. Frampton Cotterell may be made head-quarters by the fly fisherman on the Gloucestershire Frome.

CHAPTER V

THE BERKSHIRE STREAMS

THE Berkshire streams which will come under notice are the Kennet, with its tributaries, the Lambourne and the Emborne, and the Pang, a small tributary of the Thames. All four streams water the southern part of the county. The Loddon is also in the south, with a small tributary or two, but it is only in its upper parts in Hampshire that it deserves mention as a trout stream. In the north there is the Ock, flowing through the Vale of the White Horse country. It contains some good trout, I believe, in two or three of its many branches, but it is essentially a coarse fish water, and Ock pike were long ago celebrated for their alleged special excellence of flavour. It was in the county of Berkshire with its chalk hills and clear waters that the late Thomas Hughes laid some of the scenes of that popular book, *Tom Brown at Oxford*. Like his friend Charles Kingsley, a keen angler, he was very fond of the chalk streams of the counties near London. The "Englebourne" may remind the angling reader of *Tom Brown at Oxford* of either the Emborne or the Lamborne.

The Kennet, indeed a famous trout stream, takes its rise, not in Berkshire, but North Wilts. I **The Kennet** shall deal with it, however, in the present chapter. The stream rises near East Kennet, and at Marlborough, five miles down, is a splendid trouting water. Here is the Savernake fishing, preserved by the Marquis of Ailesbury. The trout are plentiful, and the average weight of those killed is, according to the fishing book, no less than two pounds. The grannom comes on in April, together with the duns common to chalk streams, but there is no May-fly to speak of on the upper reaches of the Kennet above Stitchcombe. There is not often such a failure in the water supply as to militate seriously against fishing, and the stream, which is clear and pure, is well adapted to the dry fly. The Savernake water is not re-stocked, as there is no scarcity of trout, and the coarse fish are limited to a very few dace. Altogether this is a fine piece of trouting water, flowing through a charming country. Below comes the water of Sir Francis Burdett, at Ramsbury. Here the fish, though numerous, both in the main stream and in its various branches and side streams, do not run so big. Re-stocking has been regularly carried on at Ramsbury, and the head of trout carefully kept up. Sir Francis Burdett has about five miles of the main stream. At Chilton Foliatt and by the noble old Tudor house, Littlecot, once the home of " Wild Will Darell," of sinister fame, the Kennet is seen at its loveliest, and from there downwards the trout run large. At Hungerford, just below Chilton, there was for many years an angling club of note, and the May-fly season was sometimes productive of great sport. The club

had in addition to the main stream a length of the
Dun, a small tributary flowing into the Kennet at
this point, and rising near Shalbourne. The " marsh
meadows " sometimes afforded pleasant sport when
no fin stirred on the larger water. A few years
ago the club migrated to the Wylye, and the water
reverted to the Corporation. For some reason or
other sport had become very poor out of the May-
fly season, but since then the fish seem to have
risen at the artificial fly a little more freely. There
are some very good grayling at Hungerford, but
they are not free risers at any time of year.
Below Hungerford, Kintbury, and Hampstead Park
belonging to Lord Craven, are both noted for big
trout, and in Mr. Lloyd Baxendale's water,
close to Newbury, a five-pounder is by no means
out of the common. But in these big waters there
is scarcely any rise at the small fly, and the May-
fly season is the great time. The river is broad as
well as deep in parts, and I have more than once
seen anglers wielding a double-handed twelve foot
rod for casting the dry May-fly to the rising fish—
scarcely a very delicate style of angling.

The Kennet is navigable up to Newbury, and
below that town the river is rather one for coarse fish
than for trout. The fly is not often very successful
below Newbury, the trout being large and few and
far between. Between Aldermaston and Padworth
Mills Mr. Keyser has stocked the river with two-
year-old fish—in the seasons of 1894-5, he put in
800 trout of that age—but very few of these have
so far been taken. One trout of 6 lbs. was killed
in 1897 in this water, and other large ones have
been seen. Coarse fish abound, the pike running
to a great size—seventeen or eighteen pounds—

and it is found very difficult to successfully get
them out by netting. Here, as elsewhere on the
lower Kennet, the artificial fly is not of much
service as a lure for the trout. The angler's headquarters on the Kennet are Marlborough, Ramsbury, Hungerford, where there is a capital old
angling inn—The Three Swans, Kintbury, Newbury, and Aldermaston. The Swan Inn, just
outside Newbury, is made headquarters by a
good many anglers who fish the Newbury Fishing
Association's waters on the Kennet and Lambourne. It is a comfortable and clean house, if a
small one.

The Kennet has long been famous for its fish.
Evelyn wrote of it as being "celebrated for its
troutes," and Pope alludes to the stream as "the
Kennet swift, for silver eels renowned." The old
Kennet trout was, and still is, an exceptionally
handsome fish, often golden-hued and always with
a fine red flesh. The trout of the little Dun are
also very pretty, and I have taken some late in the
season as bright almost as copper. But of course
many strains alien to the river have been introduced in re-stocking.

The Lambourne is a beautiful trout stream
flowing into the Kennet a mile below Newbury and
The Lam- close to the Swan Inn. It rises near
bourne Lambourn and has a course of twelve
miles, passing the villages of Eastbury, East
Garston, Great Shefford, Boxford and Donnington.
Rare among rivers, the Lambourne has more
water in summer than in winter, a fact first
mentioned by Best in his work on angling published
a hundred years or so since. All through the
summer there is a good stream in the higher

THE KENNETT, SAVERNAKE.

reaches between Lambourn and Shefford, but about
the middle of September the water gets lower and
lower, till, finally, about the middle of October it
disappears altogether, and the bed of the Lambourne forms the playground of the village
children till next season! Below Shefford the
water runs low but does not quite vanish.
Consequently there is no fishing to speak of higher
up stream than Shefford. In February the water
begins to rise again. The cause of this peculiarity
is well understood by geologists, though it has
been much mystified by ingenious theories about
syphons, underground passages, and the like. The
springs, as the Rev. B. T. Thompson of Eastbury
points out to me, run after rainy seasons, and are
simply the overflow of surplus water from the
chalk. From Shefford downwards the fishing is
excellent; indeed that part of the river which flows
from Shefford through Weston, Welford Park,
and Easton to Boxford can hardly in its way be
surpassed. The trout, which are paler in flesh
than those of the Kennet, are decidedly plentiful.
The fish killed would average about 1 lb., and fish
over 2 lbs. are rarely met with, despite village
traditions of four- and five-pounders. In the lower
Lambourne the May-fly season is sometimes a
fairly good one, and there is a big hatch of the
grannom on this water, as on the Kennet. A small
alder is an excellent fly on this stream, and so in
the summer evenings is the sedge. The various
dry fly patterns of the duns are all used, and
wet fly anglers find the palmers, and cowdung fly
useful. The coachman is also, like the sedge, good
towards night. There are no angling clubs

on the Lambourne, with the exception of
the piece of water fished by the Newbury
Association, and most of the fishing is rented
annually from the farmers. The Swan at Shefford
and the Bell at Boxford may be made headquarters.

The Lambourne flows through some most picturesque scenery. The higher country above the
Lambourne valley is well wooded, and the thatched
cottages with their quaint gardens and the farm
houses are a delight to the eye. The stream is
clear and pure, running through chalk and gravel.
Near Lambourn village on the chalk hills is
Wayland Smith's cave made for ever famous by
Scott in *Kenilworth*, and also the celebrated "blowing stone," of mysterious origin. It is a land
worth exploring. The Priory at Donnington, I
may add, with its delicious old-world gardens
through which the stream flows, is one of the most
pleasant spots an angler could desire to see.

The Enborne or Emborne rises in West Wood-
hay, not far from the remote Inkpen Beacon and
Coombe Hill, and for some miles, flowing
through the chalk, forms the boundary
between Hampshire and Berkshire. A
mile or two from Newtown it receives a
small tributary, and then flows to Greenham Common, from which place to the Kennet is known
locally by the name of the Anburn. Four miles
down from Newtown (which may be made headquarters) it is swelled by another brook that rises
at Kingsclere. It then passes Midgham and enters
the Kennet at Aldermaston. The stream is somewhat
neglected, at any rate in its upper parts, and trout,

The En-
borne
or Em-
borne

owing to poaching and other causes, are not very numerous. Its supply of water is not so certain as that of the Lambourne, and in many places it is overgrown with weeds and overhung with trees and bushes. Yet it might be made an excellent trouting water by means of dams here and there, and by clearing away some of the vegetation. The trout of the Enborne are decidedly good to eat, though they run at present rather small—a ¾ lb. fish being above the average about Newtown and Greenham. A gentleman who has fished the stream for 38 years tells me that he has found the minnow or a bright fly most effective. The governor, coachman, or red spinner may be used, and in the season the May-fly, which, however, is not very plentiful on this stream. A few pike and other coarse fish frequent the stream, together with plenty of minnows on which the trout feed. There are no clubs on the Enborne.

The Pang, a very pretty trout stream, rises above Frilsham, and after a course of about twelve miles joins the Thames at Pangbourne. On its way it passes Bucklebury, Bradfield, and Tidmarsh. The Pang is, in my opinion, an admirable water for the dry fly angler, but trout may, early in the season and high up stream, be taken with a cast of wet flies. In a small tributary or two I have taken them both with dry and wet fly about May-fly time, using the former in the still water and the latter in the stickles. May-fly, alder, the usual chalk stream patterns of duns, and Wickham may be used by the fly fisherman. Grayling, I fancy, have been introduced into the water, but they do not seem to have greatly thriven there.

An occasional jack may find its way up from the Thames, but there are few coarse fish above Pangbourne. The stream flows through some quiet, pretty scenery, and Pangbourne itself is still a charming village. That place or Bradfield may be made headquarters for fishing the stream.

CHAPTER VI

THE HAMPSHIRE STREAMS

THE term "Hampshire trout streams" is taken as a rule to mean Test, Anton, and Itchen, a splendid trio of waters. There are, however, some other little-known but excellent trout streams, which well deserve mention, running for the most part through a country of chalk. These are the Loddon, with its tributary the little Lyde, and the Whitewater—a tributary of the Loddon's tributary Blackwater — in the north-east corner of the county ; and the Hamble and Arle, or Meon, in the south, swelling Southampton Water. The several head waters of the Wey have been described among the Surrey Streams, and the Avon will be dealt with in the chapter on the Wiltshire streams. There are a few streams in the New Forest, such as the Boldre and the Lymington river, but they contain for the most part only coarse fish ; whilst the Beaulieu holds but a few trout, and those of a small size. The Isle of Wight streams are not of importance to the fly fisherman though the Brading and one or two other smaller waters contain a few trout.

II

The Test, formerly known as the Anton, is the undis-
puted and undisputable queen of our south country
trout streams.   If Hampshire could boast
the Test alone, it would stand high on the
list of counties from the angler's point of view.
The Test is a pure chalk stream.   It flows through
a country, the subsoil of which is invariably chalk,
the surface soil being also in many places very
calcareous.[1]   Happily no towns of any size, save
Southampton, are situated on or very near its
banks, and it has therefore escaped considerable
pollution.   Nor have water companies made as yet
their disastrous influence felt upon its pure springs.
It flows, a limpid stream, abounding with splendid
trout, and in some places with grayling of great
size, through a land, indeed, of milk and honey in
the literal sense ; through water meadows, which in
the darkest days of agriculture have often seemed to
the distressed farmer and landed proprietor the sole
redeeming feature of an all but ruinous business ;
and by villages and hamlets, the quiet beauty of
whose surroundings the patriotic Hampshire angler
will on the whole prefer to anything the mountain
streams of Wales or Scotland have to show.

The Test

[1] So chalky are several districts on the upper Test that
the villagers' kettles get encrusted after a while with a thick
white powder.   Though the clearness and the purity of the
chalk streams are proverbial, it seems from the reports of
the Rivers Pollution Commissioners that some of the waters
flowing over the granite and non-calcareous rocks in Cornwall and Devonshire are the freest of all from solids.
Analysis of the Earme water, for instance, made a quarter
of a century ago, showed a total of only 2·48 solids, and of
the South Teign a total of only 2·53.   But these rivers
are more subject to floods than those cutting through and
running over the chalk.

THE TEST AT STOCKBRIDGE.

The true source of the Test has been described
by some writers as situated in the extreme north-
west corner of the county, by the remote little
village of Upton, and not so very far from where the
Enborne takes its rise. But this stream above St.
Mary Bourne can only be described as an occasional winter bourn. It is a good many years since
it has flowed at this point in the summer months,
and I scarcely care to reckon how long it is since
I tried for some of the big trout which had found
their way so high up as Hurstbourne Tarrant.
The perennial head waters of the Test are in Ashe
Park, near Overton. At Laverstock, about four
miles down, the stream works the mill which
supplies the paper for Bank of England notes, and
the clean and pretty little town of Whitchurch,
with its picturesque White Hart Inn, is hard by.
Cobbett, who once used to spend a good deal of
his time at Hurstbourne Tarrant, or Uphusbon,
as it was then often called, says in one of his
letters : "Whitchurch is a small town, but famous
for the place where the paper has been made for
the Borough Bank! I passed by the mill on my
way . . . I hope the time will come when there
will be a monument where that mill stands, and
when on that monument will be inscribed *The
curse of England.*" Past Whitchurch the Test flows
close to Hurstbourne Park, the fine seat of the
Earl of Portsmouth, half a mile or so below which
point the stream coming from St. Mary Bourne,
and commonly called the Bourne, joins. Next the
Test, now a fine stream, flows past Longparish, the
home of Colonel Hawker, of shooting and fishing
fame, and, with the great wood called Harewood

on its west, passes by a swampy piece of ground known as Bransbury Common. Wherwell[1] comes next, then Chilbolton, and then Fullerton Bridge, where the Anton joins, and where the upper Test may be said to end. All these names are classic ones to the ardent dry fly fisherman. But before the junction with the Anton is reached, the Test receives a ten-mile tributary which comes from Micheldever, passing Stoke Charity, Bullington, Barton Stacey, and Bransbury. The Test here runs in several branches or feeders, used for flooding the water meadows at certain seasons. Stockbridge is five miles down stream from Fullerton Bridge, and Leckford and Longstock lie between, on respectively the left and right banks of the Test. Houghton and Bossington are next reached, and at the latter place the Wallop Brook or Nine Mile Water, which comes from Upper Wallop, and which is supposed to have formerly fed no less than nine mills, where it now feeds but one, joins the stream.

"Could it be proved," says Mudie, "that the ancient mills possessed the capabilities and powers of those of modern erection, it would be strong evidence in support of the theory of those writers

---

[1] Wherwell Priory, the property of Mr. Iremonger, is one of the most beautiful places on the Test. A branch of the river goes underneath the house, and the tame trout may be fed from the drawing-room windows. Wherwell church and churchyard adjoining the Priory are not places to be neglected by the angler. The churchyard contains some evergreens worth seeing, and is a favourite resort of the golden crested wren. The box and yew hedge of the parsonage garden is a singularly perfect one, and there is some fine old oak in the interior of this "haunt of ancient peace."

who contend that the south of England was
at the time of the Conquest, more thickly,
populated than it is at present, as not only in this
district, but throughout the whole country, there
were more mills at that time than at present.   But
that they must have been small is apparent, as they
were in general erected over insignificant streams,
with an inadequate supply of water to grind a large
quantity of corn, and with machinery rude and of
little power.   The state of society at that period
sufficiently accounts for the number of mills ; there
was little communication either between towns or
villages ; families were isolated ; there was but little
trade, whilst a mill was considered as requisite to
any abbey or mansion as a brewery or bakehouse."
In these days, on the other hand, the number of
small mills is steadily diminishing on many of our
southern streams, though on some there are still
too many to please the angler.

A branch of the South Western Railway follows
pretty closely the course of the Test from Fullerton
to Southampton, and has stations at Horsebridge,
Mottisfont, and Romsey, the three principal places
on the stream below the point where the Wallop
Brook comes in.   The Test here flows through
a broad valley bounded with a low range of wooded
hills—a fresh and open country, but scarcely so
pretty, and not nearly so wild, as along the upper
parts of the stream.   A little below Mottisfont
another small tributary flows in from Lockerley.
Romsey, where what has been called the mid Test
ends, is a bright town, the largest place except
Southampton on the Test or its tributaries, and here
commences the salmon water.   The stream receives
two more tributaries below Romsey, one coming

from Landford and the other from the New Forest near Lyndhurst, and at Redbridge broadens into an estuary. Southampton is three miles down, built on a sort of isthmus formed by the estuaries of this stream and the Itchen.

I may as well deal at once with the angling in these lower waters of the Test between Romsey and Redbridge. The chief proprietors here are the Right Hon. Evelyn Ashley, of Broadlands, Romsey — where Lord Palmerston once lived — Captain Beaumont, of Testwood Hall, and Mrs. Vaudrey. The Test between these points may be regarded as the salmon portion of the stream, though as a matter of fact there are a certain number of brown trout a little below even Testwood Mill. These fish run big, and are rarely taken with any but the May-fly. The salmon fishing is very valuable, and in good seasons the fish are fairly numerous, those killed averaging about 16 lbs. a-piece. Sometimes a much heavier fish is killed, and last year a noble salmon of 38 lbs. was taken at Test-wood. The salmon fishing opens on February 1, and closes on November 1. But, besides salmon, sea trout come up the stream some way above Test-wood Mill, affording good sport with the fly about the end of July. There are no angling clubs below Romsey.

Between Overton and Bransbury trout of 2 lbs. weight are not very often taken, and in general it may, I think, be very safely stated that the average weight of the trout taken in the upper Test is not above a pound. On Mr. Melville Portal's water,[1] which is now in the hands of Mr. Archibald

---

[1] I fished Mr. Groves' length at Freefolk on May 27, 1898, and found the trout extremely numerous : Freefolk is a charming spot.

Grove, the average will be seen by the following figures :—

1894.	Total bag . . .	890 trout, weighing		800½ lbs.	
1895.	One rod's bag .	211	,,	,,	204½ ,,
1895.	,, ,,	23	,,	,,	21½ ,,
1895.	,, ,,	184	,,	,,	180½ ,,
1895.	,, ,,	106	,,	,,	95 ,,
1896.	Total bag . . .	635	,,	,,	526 ,,
1897.	One rod's bag .	56	,,	,,	57 ,,
1897.	,, ,,	137	,,	,,	104½ ,,
1897.	,, ,,	51	,,	,,	48 ,,
1897.	Total bag . . .	556	,,	,,	465½ ,,

Trout are numerous both in the Test and the Bourne, which joins the main stream a mile or so below Tufton ; and the average, save here and there, is not in excess of a pound. But a few miles below we get speedily into the regions of the two-pounders, which are far from few about Bransbury, Chilbolton, and Wherwell. The Micheldever stream, which is chiefly in the hands of two riparian owners, is a fine trouting one. The lower stretches of the mill stream, before Bransbury hamlet is reached, are rather overhung, though trout can be taken even there, and good ones too. On the Common itself this tributary is very fine, abounding in beautiful fish.

From the Common downwards the trouting on the Test is very good indeed almost everywhere, is strictly preserved, but the stream is not often re-stocked. Among the more famous spots are Chilbolton, Wherwell, Leckford, Stockbridge and Mottisfont.

At Testcombe, Mr. Henry Hammans, an old Test and Anton angler, and a keen one too, took last season, to the surprise of himself and every one who heard of it, two grayling. Grayling were

introduced from the Avon into the Test at Stockbridge during the present century, but no one
before last year ever knew that they had found
their way so far up stream as Testcombe.[1]

At Fullerton Bridge the Anton flows in. This Test
tributary has its two head waters a little north of
Andover by Enham and Foxcott villages. There
are a certain number of trout running up to as
much as $1\frac{1}{2}$ lbs. above Andover—though not now
very far above—and there are splendid spawning
grounds for the fish below what is known as Shep-
herd's Spring, which rises by Enham,[2] a fair and
leafy land. It is below Andover, however, that
the angler may expect to get fairly among the
Anton trout, which are numerous, of a good size,
and fond of fly. The hatch of olive duns on the
Anton is thought to be more distributed, as it
were, over the whole day than is the hatch on the
Test. The hatch of fly and the rise of trout, so far
as my Test experience goes, is certainly on the
waters about Longparish, for instance, a clearly
defined and a regular one. On some waters there
is a steady hatch and a rise of trout more or less
throughout the day, but the Test is not one of these
streams.

The Anton receives the Anna or Pilhill Brook
at Longbridge. This tributary, which rises at
Fyfield, contains a good many trout. They rise
to the artificial fly well, and sometimes run up to
$1\frac{1}{2}$ lbs., but they are nowadays for the most part

[1] Some fine grayling may now be seen in a hole by the
Seven Stars Inn at Fullerton.
[2] Let not the angler, who has strayed so high up stream
as this point, neglect to see the pretty little church at
Enham. It is one of the oldest in the South of England.

white in the colour of their flesh, and of an inferior quality to the Anton and Test fish.[1]

Hampshire almost demands an angling volume to itself, and I find it impossible to give any save a selection of the large quantity of notes which have been very kindly placed at my disposal by proprietors, secretaries of angling clubs, and well-known chalk stream anglers. I must return therefore to the main stream without saying more of the Anton than that its course is by Charlton, Andover, and Goodworth Clatford, three miles below which place is the Test.

The most famous angling resort on the Test is undoubtedly Stockbridge. For a considerable distance above and below the town the water is fished by the Houghton Club. This celebrated angling club takes its name from Mr. Houghton, a former lessee of the fishing rights of the Manor. Originally it was intended to be not so much a trout as a pike fishing club, and even to-day the quantity of deep water in certain parts of the stream affords only too sure harbour for the latter fish, which are occasionally taken up to a large size. The club was established in 1822, and on its lists have been some illustrious names. Sheridan visited the club, if he did not actually take much part in the angling, and Sir Francis Chantrey, who designed the figure of the trout on the Town Hall of Stockbridge that acts as a weather-cock,[2] was a member. The records of the club have been well kept, and they show that the average weight of *both* trout and grayling killed on this water has

[1] See Appendix " Pilhill Brook."

[2] I am told that it always points in the fishing season to the North !

been, as nearly as possible, 2 lbs., an average only
equalled so far as I can discover, on the Savernake
water referred to in another chapter. No fish is
taken of under 1 lb. Grayling have thriven greatly
in the Test. They came originally from Heron
Court, Lord Malmesbury's place on the (Christchurch) Avon, and I am told that Mr. Harris of
Stockbridge, the old club keeper, recollects the
arrival of the first consignment, which, he says,
were turned in at Longstock, and not, as Sir
Humphrey Davy has asserted, at Leckford. Grayling are very plentiful below the Houghton water,
and have been taken with fly up to and even over
3½ lbs. Till within quite recent years no trout
of over 5 lbs. had been taken in the Houghton
water; but there are now records of fish of
6 lbs., 7 lbs., and 8 lbs. taken near the town. In
1897 a trout of 10 lbs. was taken in the main
river with a piece of bread, and another of the
same weight was taken on a trimmer at Bossington,
below the club water.

Among the principal fishing proprietors and
lessees of the Test are, beginning at its upper
waters, the following:—Colonel Bridges, Mr. Mel-
ville Portal, the Whitchurch Club, Lord Portsmouth
—who owns the greater part of the Bourne—Mr.
Watney, Lieutenant Hawker, Mr. Hammans, Mr.
Hodgson, Major Turle, Mr. Silva, Mr. Iremonger,
Mr. East, Mr. Longman, the Houghton Club, Mr.
Whitaker, Mr. Deverell, Sir A. Webster, Mrs.
Vaudry, Mrs. Thurston, Mr. Dutton, Mr. Griffiths,
Mr. Montgomery, Mr. Mortimer, Mr. Spiller, the
Rt. Hon. Evelyn Ashley, and Captain Beaumont.
The chief clubs are The Whitchurch and The
Houghton—the latter consisting at the present

time of seventeen members—and both re-stock their stretches of the river.

The dry fly method of angling is now practically universal on the Test and its tributaries, though I have heard quite recently of wet fly fishermen doing well at times on the Anton, as well as on the Test in rough weather. The olive or blue dun is the most abundant fly found on the Test, as indeed it is on all the chalk streams, but the iron blue dun, the little May dun, and the turkey brown all hatch out at times pretty freely, and only last May-fly season I found the trout feeding well for a while on all three of these *ephemeridæ*.

For artificial flies, the chalk stream patterns as tied by Farlow, Holland, Mrs. Ogden Smith, and others are in general use, and the smaller the fly the better the chance of the angler. The Test is a difficult stream, no doubt, but it has been my lot to angle in various waters quite as hard, if indeed not harder, in both the north and south of England.

The May-fly, which appears in early June, does not by any means come on in all parts of the Test and its tributaries. At Laverstock, for instance, it is unknown at the present time, though plentiful a mile or so below Longparish.[1] In regard to the lower portions of the Test, Major Carlisle informs me that the insect does not appear in any quantities till Compton and Kimbridge are reached, and that the latter is the best place.

[1] The May-fly is unknown on the upper waters of the Anton; and it is rarely seen above Gavel Acre on the Test, or above Bransbury Mill on the Micheldever branch of the Test.

" The May-fly round Stockbridge," Mr. Norman, of the Houghton Club writes to me, " began to decrease about twenty years ago, or just about the time when the canal was converted into the Andover and Redbridge Railway, and this is thought by some people to be the cause of the diminution in numbers of the insect. May-flies are still very scarce round the town, and all attempts to re-introduce them have hitherto failed, though there are plenty now below this place. The grannom entirely disappeared in the lower water. A few years ago some gallons of eggs were collected in the upper water and turned in below, with the result that the grannom is now plentiful all over the river."

I may mention the following places as good headquarters for the Test angler :—Overton, Whitchurch (" White Hart "), Hurstbourne Priors (for Bourne—" Portsmouth Arms "), Longparish (" Plough "), Bransbury (" Crook and Shears "), Bullington (for Micheldever branch of Test), Fullerton (for Anton and Test), Andover (for Anton —" White Hart," " Star," or " Junction Hotel "), Stockbridge (" Grosvenor Hotel "), Mottisfont, Romsey.

The Itchen is, next to the Test, the most famous chalk and dry fly stream in the South of England.

The Itchen   The Itchen rises a little south of Cheriton Village and runs north to Alresford. It then turns west and receives a small tributary called the Arle which rises by Brown Candover and flows through Lord Ashburton's place, Grange Park. After receiving this stream, the Itchen runs by Itchen Stoke, Itchen Abbas, Martyr Worthy, and Abbots Worthy to Winchester. For a few

THE ITCHEN AT ITCHEN ABBAS.

miles above the town, and during its entire course
below Winchester to Southampton, the Itchen flows
in several branches and is navigable between these
two places. The more notable places on the stream
below Winchester are St. Cross, beautiful Twyford,
which has been called "the Queen of Hampshire
villages," and Bishopstoke.   Hursley, once the
home of Keble, lies on the opposite side of the
Itchen to Twyford, and is three miles or so from
the water.   Below Bishopstoke is Stoneham, where
a small tributary joins containing some coarse fish
and sometimes a few salmon ; after which the
Itchen broadens into its estuary.

The chief proprietors and holders of fishing on
the Itchen and its tributaries are :—Lord Ashburn-
ham, of the Grange, Alresford ; Colonel Auburton,
at Alresford ; Captain Hewson, at Avington ; Lord
Northbrook, and Sir Edward Grey, at Itchen
Abbas ; Mr. A. Wynne Corrie, at Worthy ; Mr.
Simonds, at Abbots Barton.   Immediately below
Winchester is Chalkley's subscription water, for
which daily tickets may be obtained.   At St.
Cross, Mr. H. E. Gribble is the chief owner.   Then
come Mr. W. C. Daniels ; Mr. W. F. Flight (Twyford); Sir William Pearce, Mr. Tankerville Chamberlayne, M.P., and Sir Samuel Montagu, M.P.   Sir
Samuel Montagu's water is at Sconthing, where
there are salmon as well as trout.   At Itchen Abbas
there is a small club ; whilst a limited number of
rods, at a subscription of £20 a year, fish Mr.
Tankerville Chamberlayne's water at Bishopstoke,
where the trout and grayling run up to 3 lbs. in
weight.   There is a small piece of free water above
Winchester, including Deangate mill tail, where the
celebrated 16 lbs. 2 oz. trout was captured in July,

1888,[1] and " The Weirs " ; whilst all the rest of the river, from source to sea, is strictly preserved. Generally speaking, the fish above Winchester run rather heavier than those below ; above they are considered sizeable if 1 lb. in weight, and below if ¾ lb. There are no grayling, I believe, above Shawford. and below these fish run up to 3 lbs. The true Itchen trout are pink-coloured in flesh when boiled, but owing, no doubt, to the introduction of yearlings from other streams, there are now a good many white ones. The May-fly is plentiful in parts of the stream,[2] and the fish take it, as a rule, pretty well in the first week in June. Dry fly is now almost invariably practised on the Itchen, but in rough weather the wet fly is sometimes effective.

Among the common patterns of flies used are the olive dun, dark hare's ear, yellow dun, apple-green —a famous (Derbyshire) Wye fly—sedges, white moth, red ant, blue quill, March brown, Wickham fancy, olive quills, Flight's fancy, red quill, jenny spinner, blue-winged olive, little Marryat, ginger quill and badger quill. The cinnamon quill, claret spinner, furnace, Hammond's favourite, orange tag, red tag, and claret bumble are among the grayling flies.

The angler may make his headquarters at Alresford for the upper, Winchester for the middle, and Bishopstoke for the lower portions of the Itchen. Anglers who are interested in natural history, and especially in ornithology, will be

---

[1] This huge trout was killed one evening by a townsman angling with a plain hazel rod and with a minnow as bait, after a struggle which lasted a matter of hours. Some great fellows have also been taken from the Alresford ponds.

[2] It is rarely seen above Chilland.—ED.

THE ITCHEN AT ITCHEN STOKE.

delighted with Mr. Chalkley's museum at Winchester. It contains specimens of the spotted crake (*Crex porzana*) obtained at Chilbolton on the Test, the little gull (*Larus minutus*) obtained on the lower Itchen, together with a peregrine falcon (*Falco peregrinus*), and one or two bitterns (*Botaurus stellaris*) coming from the banks of the same stream.

The Hamble's course as a trout stream is a very short one. It rises at Bishops Waltham and runs to Botley, a distance of about four miles. The tide comes up to Botley Mills where the Hamble is seen " swelling from an inconsiderable stream to a broad estuary." This estuary, described by an old writer as "a handsome proper flood," is some nine miles long, and at one time a large number of sea trout used to come up it, some of them running to 4 lbs. and 5 lbs. The number of these fish visiting the Hamble is now sadly reduced, as they have been caught with a small mesh net by the villagers, so there are but few sea trout left in the Hamble, and they do not as a rule run large. The stream, however, contains a fair head of trout which run rather small for a Hampshire water, seldom attaining anything like 2 lbs. in weight.

The May-fly comes on in early June, and that fly and the duns and the alder are among the best lures. The wet and dry fly may both be practised. The Hamble is clear and rapid, except where the water is dammed up to make a mill head, and there it is clear and slow-flowing. It contains a few pike and roach, and in the tidal water, in addition to sea trout there are some mullet and bass. The stream flows through a country of pasture and woodland, and in many places is overgrown with alders. There are no clubs on this water, which is entirely in the hands of private individuals. I am told by a friend who formerly knew the district that the woodcock nested now and again on the banks of this stream ; but that was many years since.

The Arle or Meon is a pretty and but little known trout stream, rising at East Meon and The Arle running by West Meon, Exton, Drox-or Meon ford, Wickham, and Titchfield, where it divides into two streams, formerly called the Old River and the New River. A few miles lower down it enters Southampton Water. The direction of the Arle is almost exactly similar to the direction taken by the Test and the Itchen. It flows first in a westerly direction, and then turns gradually round and flows south to Southampton Water. The three streams, of which the Arle is by far the smallest, flow parallel with one another, the Itchen being in the middle, and the distance which separates the Test from the Itchen and the Itchen from the Arle is, as the crow flies, nowhere much more than ten miles, and sometimes less. The Arle flows through some very pleasant scenery, which is particularly pretty about the village of Wickham. From the hills around Wickham there is a fine view of the Solent and the Isle of Wight on a clear day, and altogether this is a country worth seeing. Above Wickham the Arle, which may certainly be described as a chalk stream, is small and very much overgrown in parts. The best of the trouting is, perhaps, between the village and Titchfield.

Sport on this stream is not what it once was

owing to various causes—pollution and poaching among others—but good baskets are often made. A friend tells me his bag of trout for the 1897 season was well over a hundred and fifty brace. He did particularly well evening fishing, and, indeed, after the first half of June and the disappearance of the May-fly, as a rule, found it, of little good fishing in the day-time. Dry fly may be used on the Arle ; and, as in the case of the other Hampshire chalk streams, the olive dun comes on in fair quantities. From what I have seen of the stream, I should certainly recommend the usual chalk stream patterns that are used on the Test and Itchen. The March brown is also used by some Arle fly fishermen. Mr. Goble, of Fareham, so long known as the honorary secretary of the Titchfield Fishing Club, has kindly shown me an interesting old record of fish and fishing on the Arle.[1] Salmon and sea trout appear to have been quite abundant in this stream fifty years or so since, as they were in the Hamble ; whilst lampreys also abounded below Titchfield.

The Loddon in its lower parts in Berkshire, though it contains a few large fish and has here and there been stocked to some extent, The Loddon is not really a trout stream ; but in its upper waters in Hampshire it is well worthy of notice. The Loddon is here a loam and gravel stream, rising in Newram Springs, near Basingstoke, and receiving the Blackwater at Swallowfield, where Clarendon wrote his *History of the Rebellion*. The Blackwater was once a trout stream, but now it is scarcely fit for any fish, owing to the Aldershot sewage. Its tributary the

[1] See Appendix " Arle."

I

Whitewater is happily untouched so far by the
curse of pollution, and it is possible to include it
in our list of English trout streams. From Swallowfield to Twyford is nine miles by the Loddon, but
this part of the stream need not be considered.
The trout are plentiful enough on the upper
Loddon, where the stream has been well stocked
and preserved. The limit is 1 lb. and occasionally
a fish as heavy as 4 lbs. is taken. There is a dearth
of water flies on this stream, and only in May-fly
time do the fish rise really well at the artificial.
There are no angling clubs on the Loddon, which
ten miles from its source flows through Strathfield-
saye the Duke of Wellington's place.

The Loddon was the subject of one of the
sonnets of Warton, who was born near its source,
and who addresses it as his " sweet native stream."
Pope wrote of the " Loddon slow, with verdant
alders crowned," and several of Miss Mitford's
scenes were laid on the banks of this river.

The Lyde is a tributary of the Loddon, rising
by Monk Sherborne and flowing by Pamber and
The Sherfield Green, which place the angler
Lyde may stay at. It flows through a loamy
country, and is strictly preserved. Trout are
plentiful in the Lyde, averaging about 1 lb., the
largest fish scaling 3 lbs. There is a fair hatch of
May-fly, but a scarcity of other water insects.
The Lyde, which is a very small stream, is not
fished by any angling club. It joins the Loddon
a little below Sherfield Green.

The Whitewater rises at Grewell, near Odiham,
and is swelled at Heckfield, eight miles down, by
a stream for Fleet Pond, a large sheet of water
which the main line of the London and South-

Western Railway skirts. A couple of miles below Heckfield the Whitewater joins the Blackwater,. which shortly afterwards in its turn joins the Loddon. Trout are not very plentiful on the Whitewater, but they run to a good size. Dr. Comber, who knows these waters well, tells me that there are a fair number of fish of 1 lb. and 2 lbs., and that a trout has been killed as heavy as 4 lbs. The May-fly comes on, and among the flies used by the angler are the imitations of the various chalk stream duns, the spinners, the alder and the March brown. Mattingley may be made headquarters. The Whitewater is strictly preserved, and has no angling clubs. In its upper part it may be described as a chalk stream, but lower down it flows through loams and gravel. Charles Kingsley lived in the district watered by the Loddon, Whitewater and Blackwater, and I believe frequently angled in them.

The White water

CHAPTER VII

THE DORSETSHIRE STREAMS

" PASSING through the plains and valleys," wrote Coker of the Dorsetshire streams, "they do at the last, in the most loving manner, unite themselves, and of their many branches make two big-bodied streams, Frome and Stour, both passing full of fish." The Frome and the Stour, with their tributaries, are certainly the chief waters of Dorsetshire, though there are a few other short streams flowing south into the English Channel, such as the Char, the Brit, and the Asker. The Stour is not a trout stream, though it contains an odd trout here and there, often of a good size. It has some trout, however, up towards its source, which consists of several springs in Wiltshire, and two or three of its tributaries are more or less trout-bearing. The Lidden of the Upper Stour has trout, as has the Allen or Wim of the lower; but the Develish, Tarrant, and other streams which swell the Stour are scarcely worth considering. The Frome is the largest river of Dorsetshire, but its tributaries are, with the exception of the Cerne, of little importance. It runs into Poole Harbour, as does the

Piddle or Trent, which is the third largest of the rivers of this county.

The Frome rises in two branches, one coming from St. John's Spring, near Evershot, while the other, which is sometimes called the Hooke, or Owke, comes from Hooke; the two branches unite at Maiden Newton. Near Bradford-Peverell, the stream divides itself into several branches, like the Colne in Middlesex and Buckinghamshire, "making an island of many fair and fruitful meadows." These branches unite at Dorchester, which is nine miles down from Maiden Newton. After leaving Dorchester, the Frome again divides itself, and runs in several branches to Moreton. Wool and Wareham are passed, and two miles below the latter town the Frome empties itself into Poole Harbour. Its course as a whole is rather by bold down and wild heath than through a richly wooded country. It is a clear stream, and not a very rapid one. The best trouting on the Frome is at or near Dorchester. The Dorchester Fishing Club is limited to twenty-four members, and to six privileged rods, who pay a small yearly subscription; and the latter are residents of the town. Members are not allowed to introduce friends to the water during the May-fly season—May 22nd to June 17th—but, as a matter of fact, the May-fly is no longer of much account here, having greatly decreased of late years. The club permit two 7s. 6d. tickets to be issued every day to officers stationed at Dorchester, Weymouth, and Portland, and occupiers of land abutting upon the stream have the right to issue six-day tickets during the season, the May-fly season excepted. The trout limit is eleven inches, the artificial fly

alone is permitted, and wading is only allowed
provided the fisherman keeps close in to the banks.
This last rule is a most wise one. Nothing is more
unsportsmanlike than indiscriminate wading in
chalk streams, which often disturbs the water and
sets down rising trout for hours. The season on
the club water begins on April 1st and ends on
September 30th, and the angling hours are 6 A.M.
to 9 P.M. The club has six miles of the Frome,
three above and three below the town. The trout,
which are mostly pale coloured in flesh, run from
¾ lb. to 2½ lbs., while now and then a bigger one is
taken on this river, and I have a record of one
weighing as much as 7 lbs., taken in September,
1897. Dry and wet fly fishing are both practised
on the Frome, but the former is far the more
successful method, as the trout are shy and hard
to deceive.

Of the flies the olive dun is the favourite, as it is,
and well deserves to be, on so many dry fly waters.
The stream has not been much restocked, but it is
well preserved, and its pike are fortunately few in
number. The other coarse fish are roach and dace,
and these are far from numerous. Salmon and
sea trout formerly used to go up the Frome in
considerable numbers, but, being taken out of
season, they greatly dwindled. More stringent
regulations have now been put into force to pre-
vent this barbarous practice. The tide, when high,
flows three miles above Wareham to Holme Bridge.
The Frome has a Fishery District, which includes
all streams flowing into the sea between Portland
Bill and the Hampshire boundary.

The Cerne, a nice chalk stream, joins the Frome
at Dorchester. It rises near Minterne Magna and

receives the overflow and drainings of several ponds during its course of nine miles or thereabouts. The stream is narrow, clear, and rather **The** rapid, and the banks, overgrown with **Cerne** bushes and vegetation, make fly fishing difficult in many parts. A large quantity of the water is taken up at times for the purpose of irrigating the meadows, but there are plenty of trout of an excellent quality, averaging 1 lb., and running occasionally up to twice that weight. The Cerne contains no fish besides trout, and it is not restocked. There is no May-fly, and the favourite artificials are blue upright, orange dun, yellow dun, March brown, cowdung, and red spinner; whilst the coachman has been found killing on June and July evenings about dusk. The usual method of fishing is with the wet fly. There are no clubs on this stream, and the water is all preserved by the riparian owners and occupiers. Godmanstone or Dorchester may conveniently be made headquarters by anglers who have permission to fish the upper or lower lengths of the Cerne.

The Piddle or Trent, a good trout stream, rises not far from the centre of the county in a mill pond near Piddletrenthide, and runs sixteen **The** miles to Wareham. It passes by Puddle- **Piddle** town (where it receives a tributary) Affpuddle, and Upper Hyde. The Piddle runs for the most part through a land of water meadows, and has some pretty well-wooded scenery at various points. It may be described as a chalk stream, and is very weedy in its upper parts. About Puddletown the stream has hatches, with deep holes, at intervals, and it depends a good deal on these hatches how the river will fish. When they are up, the water soon slips away, leaving little but weeds and gravel ; when they are down, good sport may often be obtained. The stream is narrow at Puddletown, but lower down it widens considerably, and becomes a good dry fly water. Among the principal proprietors are Mr. Charles Radcliffe, of Wareham, Mr. Ashton Radcliffe, of Tolpuddle, and Colonel Hibbert of Moreton. There are at the present time no angling clubs on the stream, which is well preserved by the riparian owners. Trout are plentiful, running up to a good size—3 lbs., 4 lbs., and occasionally even 5 lbs. These big fish do not often rise at fly out of the May-fly season, but trout up to 2 lbs. and a little over rise well. For dry fly fishing the olive dun, alder, sedge—which is abundant on this stream—silver sedge, yellow dun, and Wickham fancy should not be forgotten by the angler, whilst the blue upright, red upright, red spinner, silver twist, red palmer, and coachman are among the lures of the wet fly fishermen. The May-fly is variable on this water ; some years it hatches in abundance and is taken greedily by the fish, but during the last two seasons it has been a failure. There are some pike and dace in the lower portion of the stream, but, besides trout, only eels and minnows in the upper stretches.

The Britt in the south-western end of the county rises in a mill pond close to Beaminster, and is **The** eight miles in length. It passes Bridport, **Britt** two miles below which town is the sea. The little stream, like the Cerne, is somewhat difficult to fish owing to its being much overgrown. Trout are fairly numerous, and average under rather than over half a pound. The blue upright and other flies used for the Cerne will kill in this stream, as will the palmer and various Devonshire patterns. There are no angling clubs, and the water is preserved by the owners and occupiers. The Britt contains gudgeon, and no other coarse fish.

The Asker is a tributary of the Britt, and is about six miles long. It rises near Porstock, and joins the Britt at Bridport. Like that **The Asker** stream, it is much overgrown in parts and difficult to fish. Trout are more numerous in the Asker than in the Britt, but they run smaller, about three to the pound. The Asker contains no fish save trout. Flies—the same as those used for the Britt.

The Char rises in the Pilsdon Hills, and, flowing through the deep clay Vale of Marshwood, enters the parish of Whitchurch Canonicorum, **The Char** following the narrow valley between the high lands, and dividing the parish of Whitchurch Canonicorum from that of Catherston Leweston, the former being on the left bank of the stream, and the latter on the right. The Char next enters the parish of Charmouth, where it flows into the sea, after it has been increased by a tributary stream called the Wotton, which flows through the parishes of Wotton Fitzpaine and Catherston Leweston. It is a rather sluggish stream, running through clay, and presents a succession of still pools and short rapids. A few years ago the fishing was extremely poor. The trout were of a good size, running up to about 1¼ lb., but far from plentiful, in wretched condition, and of a black colour. Colonel Buller, who is the chief riparian owner, placed a good number of yearlings and two-year-old fish in the water for several years running, and as a result the fishing is now much improved. Trout are fairly

plentiful, averaging something between a quarter
and half a pound, and it is not uncommon for a
small basket to average in the month of July half
a pound a fish.   Red and black palmers, March
brown, blue uprights, iron blue dun, and hare's ear,
are the flies which appear to kill best.   The Char
contains a few eels, but no other coarse fish.
There are no angling clubs, and the water is all in
private hands.

The Shreen is a tributary of the Upper Stour,
which it joins at Gillingham, some six miles below
The Stour Head Pond.   The Shreen, which
Shreen rises at Mere, has only a short course, but
its trout are plentiful.   Fish run up to 2 lbs., and
within the last four years several much larger ones
have been obtained, three of these weighing respec-
tively $4\frac{1}{4}$ lbs., 5 lbs., and $6\frac{1}{2}$ lbs.   The water is fished
by the Gillingham Fishing Association, which allows
other lures besides the artificial fly, and has a ten-
inch trout limit.   The Association's season for
trout is from April 1 to September 30 inclusive,
and the use of the spinning minnow is restricted to
the period between August 1 and September 30
inclusive.   The favourite flies would seem to be
alder, willow fly, and Wickham fancy.   The Shreen
flows slowly through a rather flat country, and it
contains perch, roach, and dace.   The stream was
restocked with the first-named fish a few years ago.
The angler's headquarters are at the Phœnix Inn,
Gillingham.   From Gillingham the Upper Stour
and the Lidden—formerly, by reason of its leaden,
sluggish waters, called the Ledden—may be fished.
Both streams contain some good fish.   The waters
in this part of Dorsetshire have perhaps been
somewhat neglected.

The Lidden contains a fair number of trout, running from ½ lb. to 2 lbs., there being not many of the latter weight.   This stream rises in **The** Stoke Mill, and is about six miles in **Lidden** length.   It receives a small tributary, and joins the Upper Stour above Sturminster.   In addition to trout, the stream contains perch and roach.

The Allen, or Wim, is a tributary of the Stour, which it joins at Wimborne.   It takes its rise in St. Giles Park, near Cranborne, and is **The** swelled by the overflow of a considerable **Allen** sheet of water at More Critchell.   From High Hall, the residence of Canon Bernard, to Lord Shaftesbury's seat, Wimborne St. Giles, the Allen is pretty well stocked with trout, running to a good size, 3 lb. and 4 lb. fish being now and then taken in this water.   At Stanbridge the Allen has been restocked by Captain Glyn, and the whole stream is now carefully preserved from about a mile above Wimborne.   A few large trout often come up from the Stour to a pool in the town, where, as a rule, they fall victims to a lobworm. The flies for the Allen are the olive dun, iron blue dun, red palmer—a favourite—blue upright, and coachman for evening fishing.   Natural fly is scarce, and a really good hatch seldom seen on this stream.   There are no angling clubs on the Allen, and leave is not easy to obtain.   The upper part of the stream flows through meadow land, the other portions chiefly through moorland.   The Wim is much affected by the herons of Lord Alington's celebrated heronry at Crichel, through which the stream flows.

CHAPTER VIII

THE WILTSHIRE STREAMS

As it is, Wiltshire is one of the best trouting
counties in the south of England, and, if its streams
were more carefully preserved throughout and
regularly stocked, I am inclined to think that it
would rank scarcely second even to Hampshire.
The (Christchurch) Avon, Wiltshire's principal river,
flows during a considerable part of its course due
south to the English Channel, and it is swelled on
its way by such admirable chalk streams as the
Wylye, or Wily, the Nadder, the Bourne Brook,
Winterbourne, or Porton stream, and the Ebble.
These streams may be said to water the southern
half, whilst the (Bristol) Avon, with its tributaries,
and the Upper Kennet water the northern half of the
county. In the extreme north of Wiltshire is the
Thames, or more correctly speaking, perhaps, the
Isis, with a small tributary or two, such as the Ray
and the Cole. These do not merit attention as
trout streams, though many a pleasant day's coarse
fishing in past times has the writer enjoyed in the
Cole, which used to contain plenty of chub, pike,
perch, and dace.

Near Sidbury, in the northern half of the county, is an interesting point, for here what Aubrey the naturalist called the "three several waies" of Wiltshire have their sources. First, there is not far from Sidbury the permanent source of the Kennet —the spring at Cleveancy fields is uncertain—with the German Ocean as its goal ; secondly, at Culston the Blackland Brook, which through the (Bristol) Avon flows to the Atlantic ; and thirdly, at Bishops Ganning, the source of the (Christchurch) Avon, which flows to the English Channel. As regards the chalk streams of Wiltshire, it is interesting to notice that they do not follow the course of the chalk valleys as might be expected, but flow in gorges or transverse fissures. Thus the great plain of chalk called Salisbury Plain is pierced by the Bourne Brook, the Avon, Wylye, and Nadder, which meet near Salisbury. In the same way the Chiltern Hills are pierced by the Thames, and the North Downs by the Darenth and other streams.

The (Christchurch) Avon rises, as we have seen, at Bishops Ganning, and, receiving the Wylye the Bourne Brook, the Ebble, with one or two smaller tributaries which do not call for notice, flows due south, passing Devizes, Beachingstoke, Wivelsford, Charlton, Rushall, Upavon, Enford, Haxton, Nether Avon, Figheldean, Durrington, Bulford, Amesbury, Wilsford, Great Durnford, Stratford, Salisbury, Nunton, Downton, Braemore, Fordingbridge, Ibbesley, Ellingham, Ringwood, and Christchurch, where it enters the English Channel. I am in- indebted to an excellent and well-known sportsman, the Rev. William Awdry. of Ludgershall, for

The (Christchurch) Avon

some information about this stream as well as one
or two other Wiltshire waters. The trout do not
rise much above Manningford, though occasionally
heavy fish are taken at and above Pewsey. The
trouting begins to be good at Woodbridge, where
it has been carefully preserved of recent years.
Last season there were plenty of fish in the stream,
which is much sought after by anglers down to
Stratford, near Salisbury. At Syrencot, Mr.
Knowles, a keen dry fly fisherman, about seven
years ago put in grayling—which of course further
down is a celebrated Avon fish—and they have
done very well there. For some three miles both
up and down stream from Syrencot there are now
good grayling. Forty or fifty years ago Amesbury
used to be famous for its trout, and great sport was
to be had with them in the May-fly season. Sir
Edmund Antrobus, who owns a considerable stretch
of the Avon at this point, has encouraged the pike
in past times, and it is only within the last four
years or so that an effort has been made to keep
down these fish and encourage the trout. A 26-lb.
pike has been taken out of the water near Amesbury with rod and line, and lower down stream at
Wilsford an angler only last season took fourteen
pike, averaging some 8 lbs. or 9 lbs. apiece. At
Netton an effort is being made to prepare the water
for trout. A huge haul of pike was made last year
at the first cast of the net—I am afraid to say how
many. In a few years the Avon, if this war against
the pike be continued, should be a fine trout water
above Salisbury. At present the best trouting is
between Amesbury and Upavon, where, besides Sir
Edmund Antrobus, the principal owners are Mr.
Ledger Hill, Mr. Fowle, Sir Michael Hicks-Beach,

Mr. Hussey Freke, Mr. Knowles, and Colonel Wad-
dington. I am reminded, however, that the Govern-
ment have now acquired land from Durrington
to Upavon for military manœuvres, and it remains
to be seen if the fishing, or how the fishing, will be
affected thereby. One can only devoutly hope that
the fate of the Upper Avon will not be that of the poor
Blackwater of Hampshire! The lower Avon contains of course good trout, and in parts good grayling, too; indeed it was the Avon which supplied
the Test with the ancestors of its present splendid
specimens of *thymallus*; but coarse fish abound.
Avon eels appear to have been famous many hundreds of years ago, and there is mention of them in
Doomsday, and Avon salmon are splendid fish,
running very large. The latter get up as far as
Ringwood. The Avon flows past many an interesting spot and beautiful scene. Netheravon is in
a fine sporting country, and it was here that Cobbett
was once shown "an acre of hares." Salisbury, with
its noble spire and its bright shops, is an attractive
country town, and by and by as the river begins to
wend its way by the New Forest, many scenes of
beauty disclose themselves. One of the prettiest
villages by the stream is Ibbesley in Hampshire
"with," writes Mr. Wise in his *The New Forest*,
"its cottages by the roadside, and their gardens of
roses and poppies and sweet peas, and their porches
thatched with honeysuckle. Three great elms over-
hang the river, spanned by the single arch of its
bridge; whilst the stream pours sparkling and foam-
ing over the weir into the water meadows, and in
the distance the town of Harbridge rises out from
its trees . . . . but the whole river is here full
of beauty, winding, scarce knowing where, among

the flat meadows, one stream flowing one way, and one another, and then all suddenly uniting in the shade of the trees; and being repulsed, flowing away again into the meadows, white with flocks of swans and fenced in with green hedges of rushes and yellow flags."

By the banks of the Avon, as by those of the Test, you may often find late in the summer the fine yellow loosestrife, whilst the comfrey and the buckbean, or " fringed water lily," as it is called by the country folk, flourish nearly everywhere.

The Wylye, or Wily, rises by Hill Deverill Mill, about a mile from Kingston Deverill, and for six miles or so its head waters are known as the Deverill. The name Deverill is said by some authorities and antiquaries to have come from "diving rill," it being a peculiarity of this stream that in some seasons its head waters rise irregularly to the surface of the meadows with intervals of dry turf which mark a subterranean river. Camden asserts this, as does Aubrey, the Wiltshire naturalist, but others have pointed out that Deverill probably comes from the Celtic *dever* or *defer*, which simply meant a stream. The course of the Deverill is over a chalk bed, with here and there deep holes. A portion of the stream is scarcely fishable, owing to the action of mills, which occasionally take up almost all the water for their own purposes, and compel the trout to seek shelter in the holes. The Deverill indeed in parts may be regarded not so much an angling stream as a stew or receptacle for fish, which can be easily netted out when required. Above Longbridge Deverill there is, however, some fairly good fishing. The Marquess of Bath owns most of the

water to Warminster, and he has recently re-
stocked it with three hundred brace of two-year-
old trout. The fish run to a fair size ; some have
been taken up to 3 lbs., but this is of course far
above the average. They are excellent to eat, and
of a less muddy flavour than some of the fish
further down stream. There is May-fly, as a rule,
about the first week in June in the lower portion
of the Deverill, and the best artificial flies are
thought to be the red spinner, the March brown,
and the alder.

At and below Warminster, where the little Were
flows in, the stream is known as the Wylye. It
joins the (Christchurch) Avon at Salisbury after
passing Heytesbury, Codford, Wylye, Wishford,
and Wilton. Its chief tributaries are the Nadder,
which will be treated of separately, and the Winterbourne. There are several streams called Winterbourne[1] in this county and Dorset, and they are so
called because they only run, or only run fully, in
winter. The stream which comes from above
Shrewton and flows into the Wylye at Stapleford
holds, I am told, some good trout. Lord Heytesbury's water at Heytesbury is well preserved.
Trout are plentiful, running up to 2 lbs. and 3 lbs.,
whilst an occasional 4-lb. fish is taken. The fish
have the reputation of rising pretty freely—not
one nowadays by any means too common among
chalk-stream trout—and the flies commonly used
are alder, hare's ear, grannam, sedge, red spinner,
red tag (for grayling), the various chalk-stream
pattern of the duns, and the blue upright. The
river here runs through alluvial water meadows
between chalk hills, and its bed is gravel. There

---

[1] Winterbourne, nailbourne, or bourne.

K

is, at the time of writing this, water to be let near Heytesbury. The Wilton Fly-fishing Club's water is leased from the Earl of Pembroke, Mr. Stanley Leighton, Lady Herbert of Lea, and others, amounts in all to upwards of ten miles, and includes both banks. It extends from a point about half a mile above the village of Steeple Longford to the town of Wilton. The Club has four railway stations within easy distance of the water —two at Wilton (G.W.R and S.W.R), one at Wylye (G.W.R.), and one at Wishford (G.W.R.). The last-mentioned place is supposed to be particularly good for grayling. The Wilton Club have re-stocked the Wylye on an extensive scale, putting in many thousands of *fario* and *levenensis* of various ages brought from different parts of the country. They also began by re-stocking with grayling, but I do not fancy the latter experiment has been repeated ; perhaps there are too many grayling as it is in the stream. The Club rent a portion of the Berwick stream for re-stocking purposes. The season for trout commences on May 1, and ends on September 30, and the season for grayling is from July 1 to December 31, inclusive ; grayling, however, of 10 inches or less in length may be killed at any time. No trout of under 12 inches in length may be killed, and not more than four brace may be taken in a day—an excellent rule. Eight brace of grayling of over 10 inches in length may be taken in the day, and any number of grayling of under that length. The entrance fee is £20, and the annual subscription £30. Each member has every year six transferable daily tickets, and no one can become a member of the Club who resides within 20 miles

of Stoford Bridge, Wiltshire. The average weight
of the trout killed on this water would be about
¾ lb. As regards the flies, there is now only a
small hatch of May-fly where twenty years ago
there was a big one. The usual chalk-stream
patterns of duns, &c., are used, and dry fly fishing
is found, as a rule, to be the best method of tempt-
ing the trout. The stream is clear, flows at a
moderate pace, and is not greatly interfered with
by mills. The Wylye is thus referred to in
Michael Drayton's *Polyolbion* :—

" First, Willy boasts herself more worthy than the other,
And better far deriv'd : as having to her mother
Fair Selwood, and to bring up Dyver in her train ;
Which, when the envious soil would from her course
    restrain
A mile creeps under earth as flying all resort :
And how clear Nader waits attendance in her court ;
And therefore claims of right the Plain should hold her
    dear,
Which gives the town a name ; which likewise names the
    shire."

The Nadder, which has on its banks Lord
Pembroke's place, Wilton, once described by
Tennyson as " the most paradisal country   The
seat," where Sir Philip Sydney wrote his Nadder
Arcadia, rises at Shaftesbury in Nadder Head
Lake, and, flowing through some pleasant scenery,
joins the Wylye at Wilton, after passing Tisbury
and Dinton, and being swelled by the overflow of
several lakes at Wardern Park. It is scarcely so
well preserved as the Wylye, except above Tisbury,
where there is a fly-fishing club, and also near
its junction with the larger stream. Trout are
plentiful above Tisbury, where they would average
about 1½ lbs. ; below they have been occasionally

taken up to 5 lbs. in weight. There is no May-fly
season, and the red spinner is the Nadder fly in
which some anglers have the greatest faith. Hare's
ear, cow-dung, and the indispensable alder are used,
together with the chalk-stream duns. I am told
that below the junction of the Nadder with the
Wylye there are some fine grayling at Bemerton,
once the home of George Herbert the poet, where
the water is now well preserved. Tisbury, Dinton, or
Wilton may be mentioned as suitable headquarters,
the two latter places for the lower stretches of the
Nadder, and the first-named for the upper. The
club already referred to has some seven miles of
water above Tisbury.

This stream is for its first few miles sometimes
called the Don, becoming the Nadder after the
little Sem joins it at West Hatch.

The Ebble, a nice little chalk stream, rises at
Ebblesford Wake and flows into the (Christchurch)
The Avon at Longford. It is about fourteen
Ebble miles in length, and passes Broad Chalk
and Tony Stratford. There are in particular some
excellent trout as well as grayling in the mile or so
of this stream below Nanton Bridge, and just
before it joins the Avon. Flies—the usual chalk-
stream patterns of duns, &c. The Ebble is sometimes called the Chalk or Chalke Stream. Hoare
describes the Vale of Chalk as "the most
sequestered district in the county."

The Porton Stream, Bourne, or Winterbourne,
joins the left bank—the Wylye and Ebble join on
The the right bank—of the Avon at Salisbury.
Porton This stream is seldom visible above
Stream Idmiston, though about once every
eight or nine years the springs rise at Southgrove,

near Burbage, ten miles higher up. It contains
good trout, especially at the present time between
Porton and Winterbourne Earls, as well as below
Laverstoke and at Longford Castle. Though I
have seen a few good trout now and then miles
above the *ordinary* source of some streams, such as
the Hampshire Bourne, I cannot hear that any
have ever appeared above Idmiston, even when the
springs have been up. The chalk-stream patterns
and the dry fly may be used on the Porton Stream.

Before leaving this part of Wiltshire, I may
mention that there are some fine trout to be seen
at the Bridges in Salisbury. These fish run up to
a great weight. Now and again a large one is
captured, but not, it is to be feared, by a very
sportsmanlike device. The Porton Stream was not
overlooked by Drayton, who referred to it as the
" pretty Bourne."

The (Bristol) Avon and its branches and
tributaries water the north-west part of the
county. The stream rises by Tetbury, The
and passes among other places in Wilt- (Bristol)
shire, on its way to the Bristol Channel, Avon
Malmesbury, Dauntsey, Chippenham, and Trowbridge. It receives several tributaries, such as the
Thunder Brook, the Maiden, and the Biss. It is
also swelled by the drainings of several lakes, such
as Lord Lansdowne's in Bowood Park, which some
consider would make the finest sheet of water for
trout fishing in the South of England, were it
cleared of its pike and other coarse fish and stocked
with Loch Levens. The (Bristol) Avon is, on the
whole, far more in the nature of a coarse fish than
a trout stream, but it does contain trout, and good
ones too, in various stretches and in several of its

tributaries, especially in the Somersetshire ones, which are considered in the chapter on that county. Among the best places for trout are Malmesbury, where there is an angling club, Chippenham, Trowbridge, and, a friend tells me, Limpley Stoke. At Lowerford the water is actually preserved for trout, and last season some heavy fish were killed there with the May-fly. About Semington, too, the (Bristol) Avon is said to contain good trout. The nearest railway station to this place is Melksham, three miles off.

The Box Brook flows through the north-eastern corner of Wiltshire, joining the (Bristol)
The Box Brook Avon, as does St. Catherine's Brook, another trout stream, at Bathampton. The Box Brook, which is about eight miles in length, is an admirable trout stream, rising by West Kington in Wiltshire. The best stretches are at Castle Coombe and Ford, where the water is carefully preserved. The trout taken in this stream scarcely average more than $\frac{1}{2}$ lb., but they are plentiful. A 1 lb. fish is a decidedly good one. A hunting friend reminds me that it was in Slaughterford wood, by the Box Brook, that the late Mr. Collier had his celebrated run. Everybody believed he was running a fox, but the hounds killed a big dog otter of 25 lbs. just before it reached the Box Brook. Castle Coombe may be made headquarters for this water. Wet fly and dry fly can both be used.

CHAPTER IX

SOMERSETSHIRE is a fairly well watered county, having a good many rivers, some of considerable size; but it scarcely possesses any trout streams which can compare with the first-class streams of Hampshire, Wilts, Berks, or Dorset. Its chief river is the Parret, a turbid and sluggish water, running, for the most part, through a flat country, much of which is reclaimed bog and marsh, and containing a good number of pike, perch, roach, dace, carp, tench, and other coarse fish. Near its source the Parret has more the appearance of a trout stream, and some years ago it contained a fair number of trout in its head waters; but it cannot now claim to be a trout stream in any part. The Parret's chief tributaries are the Isle, Tone, Carey, and Yeo or Ivel; whilst the Brue joins the estuary of the Parrett near Highbridge. The Isle, Tone, and Carey, with some of their tributaries, contain trout; but the Yeo, or Ivel, has only a few here and there, none about Ilchester, though an occasional one, I believe, in the neighbourhoods of Yeovil and of Chilton Cantels. An interesting spot in the

county is the highway between Crewkerne and
Chard, which is the division of the watershed of
the counties of Somerset and Devonshire. The
water on the south side feeds the Devonshire Axe,
and on the north the Parret, thus flowing respectively into the English and the Bristol Channels.
At St. Reine's Hill hard by is the furthest point
west at which chalk is found.

The (Somersetshire) Axe, which takes its rise at
Wookey Hole, rushing with great force from the
cavern and soon driving several mills at the
Mendips, is not a trout stream, though one or two
proprietors have stocked the river with trout as it
runs through their grounds in the upper stretches.
Further north there are a few streams containing
trout in small numbers, such as the small Kenn.
The Frome, I believe, also has some fish here and
there, though, on the whole, they are scarce. The
Chew, which, like the Somersetshire Frome, is a
tributary of the (Bristol) Avon, is a much better
trout stream, and deserves separate notice. The
western highlands of Somerset contain a good
number of small trout streams, amongst them being
the Barle of Exmoor, and the upper parts of the
lovely Lyn. In the Quantock Hills there are some
small streams containing plenty of troutlets, such
as the Williton Brook and the Washford and the
Dunster. It is a beautiful county, and has been
described in one of Richard Jefferies's most exquisite sketches, *Summer in Somerset*: " From the
Devon border I drifted like a leaf detached from a
tree across to a deep coombe in the Quantock
Hills. The vast hollow is made for repose and
lotus-eating ; its very shape, like a hammock,
indicates idleness . . . . everywhere wild straw-

berries were flowering on the banks—wild straw-
berries have been found ripe in January here—
everywhere ferns were thickening and extending,
foxgloves opening their bells. Another deep
coombe led me into the mountainous Quantocks,
far below the heather deep beside another trickling
stream. In this land the sound of running water
is perpetual, the red flat stones are resonant, and
the speed of the stream draws forth music like
quick fingers on the keys; the sound of runn'ng
water and the pleading voice of the willow-wren
are always heard in summer. . . . There is a fly-
rod in every house, almost every felt hat has gut
and flies wound round it, and every one talks trout."

The Isle is a tributary of the Parret, which it
joins a couple of miles above Kingsbury. It rises
at Chard, and, flowing by Ilminster, which   The
can be made headquarters, receives two   Isle
or three small tributaries. The Isle is a clear and
fast stream, flowing over the lias through rich
pasturage and agricultural land, and containing
numerous trout running up to about one pound.
Fly fishing is general, and the blue uprights and
red palmers are recommended as killing flies.
Lewis, in his *Book of English Rivers*, speaking
of the source of this stream, says : " It is a remarkable fact that a stream which rises from a spring at
the west end of the principal street is easily turned
so as to run into the Bristol or the English
Channel."

The Tone, one of the Parret's most important
tributaries, rises near Clatworthy, and flows by
Wellington, Taunton, Creech St. Michael,   The
and Athelney near which town it joins   Tone
the main stream. It receives several brooks

holding trout, such as the Milverton, which comes
from near Wiveliscombe, the Norton, the Kingston,
and the Black, which joins at Taunton. Trout
run from ¼ lb. to 1 lb. in the Tone, and the chief
flies are the May-fly, March brown, February
red, blue uprights, and duns. Fly fishing and the
artificial minnow are the methods of angling, and
at Taunton there is an Association, which preserves a portion of the stream. The Tone, which
is fairly clear and rapid, flows through an undulating and well-wooded country, and in addition
to trout it contains dace, roach, eels, and other
fish. It may interest anglers who are fond of
birds and bird-life to hear that hard by Taunton
the marsh warbler (*Acrocephalus palustris*) has
more than once been found breeding. The claim
of this interesting bird to be regarded as a British
species has only been established within quite
recent years, but it has probably often enough
been taken for the far commoner frequenter of
our streams and their immediate vicinities, the reed
warbler. I have never been so fortunate as to
come across the very local marsh warbler, but do
not despair of making its acquaintance some day
during an angling excursion. Its song is said
by some to be only second to that of the Nightingale itself. Seebohm asserts that its song recalls
those of the swallow, the lark, the tree warbler,
the nightingale, and the blue throat—"not so
loud as that of the nightingale, but almost as rich
and decidedly more varied." The marsh warbler
is not to be confused with the still scarcer aquatic
warbler (*Acrocephalus aquaticus*), a specimen of
which was, I see, obtained last year at Farlington,
in south-east Hampshire.

Drayton writes of—

"The Beauteous Tone,
Crowned with embroider'd banks, and gorgeously array'd
With all the enamel'd flowers of many a goodly mead."

The Chew unites with the (Bristol) Avon at Keynsham. It rises at Chewton Mendip, and runs a course of some twenty miles, pas- **The** sing West Harptree, Chew Stoke, Chew **Chew** Magna, and Pensford. It is a somewhat sluggish and not a very clear stream, flowing through a level valley during most of its course, though much of the neighbouring country is broken and hilly. The Chew is much overhung by trees in parts, and some anglers prefer a bright minnow to the artificial fly, whilst dapping with the natural insect— either May-fly or bluebottle—is also sometimes practised. The trout are fairly plentiful, especially in the upper reaches, and run from $\frac{1}{4}$ lb. to 2 lbs., averaging perhaps about $\frac{3}{4}$ lb. The artificial flies used are the May-fly, March brown, Wickham fancy, alder and coachman. Besides trout, the stream contains perch, roach, gudgeon and eels. The stream is preserved, but leave may sometimes be obtained, and Pensfold or Chew Stoke may be made headquarters. At Chew Magna, where the stream flows through the red sandstone, the Bristol Waterworks Company have a reservoir which contains some trout, and may be fished by daily ticket.

The Barle rises by Moles Chamber in the heart of Exmoor Forest, flows past Simonsbath, Land- acre Bridge, Withypool, Dulverton, and **The** Brushford, and joins the Exe a little below **Barle** Dulverton Station. Its entire length is in Somer- setshire. The two best places—indeed, the only

places—for the angler to make his headquarters at
on the upper parts of this delightful little trout
stream are Simonsbath and Withypool. Simonsbath, where there is a comfortable inn, the William
Rufus, is reached by driving from South Molton
Station, or else from Lynmouth, which is a few
miles nearer. Sir William Knight is the chief
owner of the fishing on the upper Barle, and, if
properly approached, gives permission to anglers
staying at Simonsbath. At Simonsbath the
stream is open and easy to fish, and the troutlets
are plentiful, running from six to eight to the
pound. Between Withypool and Dulverton, the
Barle, now well wooded, flows through beautiful
scenery the whole way to its junction with the
Exe. At Torre-steps, it is perhaps seen at its best
in summertime, and here is an excellent cottage
on the hill-side where refreshment may be obtained. Dulverton is a little town on the lower
stretches of the Barle, having several hotels with
fishing rights, and a railway station. The angler
stays at the Red Lion, the Lamb, or the Carnarvon
Arms, between the town and the station, and here
the trout run larger than above. A basket containing
fish of about five to the pound may often be made,
and on the Earl of Carnarvon's water some $\frac{1}{2}$ lb.
and $\frac{3}{4}$ lb. trout occasionally rise pretty well in April
—the season begins on February 14th—to the wet
fly. Dulverton should also be made headquarters by
the angler who desires to fish—(1) the upper Exe,
which rises, like the Barle, in Exmoor Forest, and
flows by Exford, Winsford, and Exton ; (2) the
Haddeo, and (3) Brushford Brook—the two latter
being tributaries, joining the Exe on, respectively,
the left and the right bank. I use the March

brown, the blue uprights, and the Wickham as flies
for the Barle.   Towards evening a coachman is
sometimes a good lure.

The Lyn, or East Lyn, rises near Oare Oak, in
a country which Mr. Blackmore has made famous
in his romance of *Lorna Doone*, and, joined   The
by the Oare water and the Bagworthy   Lyn
water, with one or two other streams, crosses
the border and, passing Brendon, reaches the
Bristol Channel at Lynmouth.   It is not difficult
to get permission to angle in this beautiful
little stream, and visitors staying at the Bath
and the Lyndale Hotels have the right.   The
trout ordinarily taken will not be found to run
much above six to the pound, but there certainly are days when a good many bigger ones
may be taken.   A pound trout is sometimes to be
taken in the lower and wildly-wooded parts of
the stream, but minnow and worms are more likely
to kill a fish of this weight than artificial fly.
Duns, palmers, blue uprights, and the March
brown may be used, and on one or two occasions
I have found the pale evening dun a particularly
good pattern in summer time.   The coachman is
also very good on the Lyn, and some anglers never
have it off their casts.   The Lyn contains some
excellent salmon, which are taken with worms in
the late summer and early autumn.   I have never
heard of but one fish being taken with a fly.   The
stream is rapid, and below Watersmeet, which
Whyte Melville has described in his pretty
story *Katerfelto*, it has some beautiful little pools.
The Lyn here flows through a deep gorge, and
from the footpath far above, looking down at the
stream as it roars and foams from one emerald

green pool to another, one may sometimes see some fine fish waiting for sufficient water to get up. This lovely little stream has reminded me somewhat of portions of the Hemsedal of Southern Norway, especially in the wonderful green of its waters. Lynmouth is within a five-mile drive of Paracombe, where there is another small stream containing plenty of troutlets, which flows into the Bristol Channel at Trentishoe. Visitors staying at the Lyndale Hotel can fish this stream, as also portions of the West Lyn, which joins the Lyn at Lynmouth.

CHAPTER X

DEVONSHIRE may be safely described as the most troutful county in the south of England. It has far more streams than any other county referred to in this volume, and they are one and all—save where poisoned—trout producing. Many of its streams flow through wild and romantic scenery, and most of them abound in trout of a small size. Devonshire has many excellent angling inns delightfully situated, and permission to fish is by no means so difficult for the stranger or tourist to obtain as it is in the case of the chalk streams of the Home Counties. Moreover, in Devonshire the least skilful fly fisherman may commonly reckon on getting a little sport, though he must not expect to put together those baskets of four or five dozen troutlets which often fall to the lot of the accomplished and the local angler. Devonshire has such a large number of trout streams that it really requires a book to itself, but I shall endeavour within the space at my command to give some particulars respecting its best and most considerable waters. In the eastern corner there is the Axe, which rises in Somersetshire, and, swelled

by several tributaries, the chief among which is
the Yarty, which also rises in Somerset, flows into
the sea at Axmouth. Next come the little Sid
and the much more important Otter ; the Exe,
with its tributaries, the Loman, the Creedy, and
the Culm ; the Teign, with its tributary the Bovey ;
the Dart, the Avon, the Erme, the Yealm, the
Plym, the Tamar, with the Tavy—all flowing into
the English Channel ; and in the north, flowing
into Barnstaple Bay and the Bristol Channel, are
the following :—The Torridge, with its tributaries
the Waldon, the East Okement and the West
Okement ; the Taw, with its tributaries the Little
Dart, the Mole and the Yeo ; with the little
streams, the Heddon and the Lyn, in the extreme
north and close to Exmoor Forest.

The two leading Devonshire flies are the blue upright and the March brown. There is no insect called
the blue upright fly in nature, but the artificial so
named may often be identified with the blue dun,
which, by the way, I feel pretty sure is the same
as the famous "olive" of the chalk stream angler.[1]
The blue upright is used on the Windrush of
Gloucestershire, and Colonel Waller, of Bourton-
on-the-Water, has written to me in regard to this
matter : "I believe, and my opinion is corroborated
by some who have known the blue upright of
Devonshire, that it is identical with the blue dun
of this river." Mr. Austin, of Tiverton, writing to me
on the same subject, says—"The designation blue
upright is only an indefinite one, as there are four
flies that come under that name—the female
winged blue upright, the winged blue upright, the
female hackled blue upright, and the hackled blue

[1] See *The Book of the Dry Fly*, page 173.

upright ; although here it is always considered that
the blue upright means the last-mentioned. Your
Gloucestershire friend is not alone in describing
the blue upright as being identical with the blue
dun. Francis Francis was of the same opinion a
quarter of a century ago, as others have been since.
But while I am ready to admit that the winged
blue upright is not a bad copy of an early dun, I
consider that the hackled fly is an equally good
copy of the March brown." Mr. Austin adds, and
gives his reasons for holding the view, that, whatever fly the blue upright was originally intended to
be a likeness of, it is taken by the trout, not as a
fly in the winged state, but as the nympha—that
is, of course, when it is used in, not dry, but wet fly
fishing. The blue upright, whatever fly it is or was
intended to be a copy of, and whatever it is taken
by the misguided trout to be, is certainly a most
valuable lure in Devonshire, Somersetshire and
Cornwall, and I am glad therefore to be able to
give Mr. Austin's drawings of the four patterns :—

(i) *The female winged blue upright.*
    Body—Made from a peacock quill, with a
        white tip showing at end of body.
    Wings—Starling.
    Legs—Blue hackle.
    Hooks—Nos. 1 to 4.
    Tying silk—Primrose.
(ii) *The winged blue upright* (or *blue quill*).
    Body—Stripped peacock herl.
    Wings—Starling.
    Legs—Blue hackle.
    Hooks—Nos. 1 to 4.
    Tying silk—Claret.

(iii) *The female blue upright.*

> *Body*—Stripped peacock herl, tied to show a white tip to the body.
>
> *Legs and wings*—Smoky blue cock's hackle.
>
> *Hooks*—Nos. oo to 4.
>
> *Tying silk*—Claret.

(iv) *The blue upright.*

> *Body*—Peacock herl stripped.
>
> *Legs and wings*—Dark blue gamecock's hackle.
>
> *Whisks*—Same.
>
> *Hooks*—Nos. oo to 4.
>
> *Tying silk*—Claret.

Devonshire has eight out of the seventeen Fishery Districts of the southern counties. These Districts are administered by Boards of Conservators, who deal with matters relating to the close seasons for various fish, the issue of licenses, &c., and whose powers often extend to the sea for a distance of three miles from the shore, or to the mid-channel in estuaries. The Boards consist of conservators appointed by the County Councils every year, from those qualified by ownership of land or fisheries of a certain value, and of representative members, elected annually by persons who have paid license duty on instruments other than rod and line used for salmon-fishing in public waters. The Devonshire Fishery Districts are the following :—Axe (Beer Head to Portland Bill), Otter (Ottermouth to Beer Head), Exe (Clerk Rock to Ottermouth), Teign (Hope Ness to Clerk Rock), Dart (Start Point to Hope Ness), Avon (Stoke Point to Start Point), Tamar and Plym (Rame Head to Stoke Point), and Taw and

Torridge (the whole of the North Coast of Devonshire. The Cornwall Fishery Districts are :—The Fowey (Peel Point to Rame Head), and the Camel (which covers the western boundary of Devonshire to Peel Point).

I. DEVONSHIRE

The Axe is one of the most fishable of Devonshire streams. It rises near Picket Mill in Somersetshire, and, after receiving a small tributary or two, such as the Kit, and passing Chard Junction, enters Devonshire at a point two miles above Axminster. This town may be regarded as the principal headquarters of the angler on this stream, and the chief hotel is the George. Below Axminster the stream receives the Yarty, and at Colyton a tributary called the Coly, which rises at Cotleigh, and runs a course of about fourteen miles. The Axe reaches the sea at Seaton, below Axmouth. It is a clear and rapid stream, containing salmon as well as trout. At one time indeed the former fish must have been pretty abundant in the Axe, for there are old indentures still existing which stipulate that apprentices at Axminster shall not be fed on salmon more than twice a week. Trout are fairly plentiful in the Axe, and the fish killed run from ½ lb. to ¾ lb. Fly fishing is the usual method of angling, and the favourite flies are the blue upright, the red palmer, the iron blue dun, the blue dun, and the March brown. There are no angling clubs on this stream, and the fishing is mostly preserved by the owners and occupiers. The country through which the

Axe runs is a pleasant fertile one, and there is much pasture land beside the stream.

The Yarty is a gravel and loam stream, rising near Kent's Mill. It passes Yarcombe and **The** Stockland—which may be made head-**Yarty** quarters—and Kilmington, where it receives Dalwood Brook, containing a good many trout. The Yarty, after a course of thirteen miles, flows into the Axe at Axminster. It contains some salmon and salmon-peel, and is full of trout. There are a good many fish of about ¾ lb., and here and there a two-pounder may be taken. The Yarty is strictly preserved, and has no clubs. An angler who knows the water very well recommends as the best flies the duns with their *imagines* or spinners, and the alder. Dry as well as wet fly may be used.

The Otter, one of the earliest and best of Devonshire waters, rises at Otterford in the Black **The** Down Hills just inside Somersetshire, and **Otter** passes Honiton, Ottery St. Mary—which may be made headquarters—Tipton, Newton Poppleford, and Otterton, to within a mile of which place the tide flows up. The tributaries of the Otter are Pennythorn Brook, Blanacombe Brook, Awlescombe Brook, and Tailwater Brook. Trout are plentiful in this excellent fly-fishing stream. They average about ½ lb., and sometimes run up to chalk-stream size, one being indeed killed in 1896 weighing no less than 5½ lb. Fly fishing is the method of angling on the Otter, and the favourite patterns include the blue uprights, haresflax (olive and red), red upright, yellow and olive duns, and partridge quill. The Otter, which flows through a nice country of meadows and woods, is a clear, and generally a rapid stream, containing besides its trout some salmon-peel and eels. The Hon. Mark Rolle preserves the Otter from Tipton down to Clamourbridge, and there is one ticket to be had by a visitor at the Imperial Hotel, Exmouth, and one at the Rolle Hotel, Budleigh Salterton. Ottery St. Mary, a delightfully situated town, was the birthplace of Coleridge, who alludes affectionately to the Otter in one of his sonnets. The pastoral poet, Browne, too once lived at Ottery St. Mary.

The Exe is "a most beautiful river," says Skrine, "rapid in its origin, but soon disporting itself in a tranquil stream amidst verdant meadows, and surrounded by a well-cultivated district." The stream takes its rise in mid-Exmoor, in a lonely and rugged district, and enters Devonshire near Bampton. It receives the Haddeo, which Lord Carnarvon preserves, above Dulverton, and the far larger Barle at Exbridge ; and between this point and Tiverton the Brushford brook, Bel brook, and Bampton brook flow in, while the Loman joins at Tiverton. The next important points, following the stream downwards, are Bickleigh, Silverton, Thorverton, Brampford Speke and Cowley Bridge. The Dart joins the Exe at Bickleigh and the Culm near Brampford Speke. The Creedy joins below Cowley Bridge, and shortly afterwards Exeter Bridge is reached. The Exe has several angling associations. The Tiverton Angling Association fishes the water for four miles below the town ; the Upper Exe Fishery Association preserves it between Bickleigh Bridge and Thorverton, and the Lower Exe Association, from Thorverton to Cowley Bridge. In addition there is the Landowners' Salmon Fishing Association.

There is some fair salmon fishing on the Exe, though the fish are rarely up to the standard of those of Scotland or Norway, and salmon fry or samlets are sometimes as great a nuisance to the trout angler as they are on the Welsh rivers. The trouting on the water of the Lower Exe Association is scarcely worth considering. Below Thorverton Weir there are pike and other coarse fish, but only dace, I believe, above.[1] In the Tiverton water trout are plentiful, running about five to the pound above and three to the pound below. Here the duns and the March brown are the chief natural flies, and the favourite artificial are the several blue uprights, the March brown, the blue or olive and the yellow duns, half stones, and gold and silver twist patterns. Fly fishing is the usual method of angling, though worm and minnow are both resorted to at times. A good many Exe anglers believe in fishing down-stream with several flies to any other style, though up-stream fishing with a dry fly is occasionally tried with some success. Lower down stream, about Silverton and Thorverton, trout are fairly plentiful, running about six or seven ounces apiece, with here and there a fish of ¾ lb. Above Thorverton the river is pretty fast, a succession of stickles and pools, with occasional rocky places ; below Thorverton its pace is slower. The stream is ordinarily a clear one, coming down rather red in flood times. Wading is necessary in many parts. The scenery of the Exe, though fine in its desolate way in the upper parts of the stream, can

[1] Grayling have been introduced, but I have not heard with what success.

scarcely compare with that of the Dart and one or two other Devonshire waters, but it is still very charming with its richly wooded vale between Bampton and Tiverton, and its "enamelled meadows" in many a winding stretch far below that town.

The Loman, or Lowman, which joins the Exe at Tiverton, rises near Huntsham, and is swelled by a tributary at Uploman. It is nine or ten The Loman miles in length and contains a good number of trout, which run about five or six to the pound, with here and there a fish of ¾ lb. The stream is an early one, and these flies may be used by the angler :—Maxwell's blue, blue upright—the female blue upright is said to be specially good on this stream, as on the Culm—the little May dun, and the spring fly. The last-mentioned is dressed by Mr. Austin as follows :—Body—equal parts of fox's and squirrel's fur from the back ; hackle—rusty blue ; tying silk—primrose ; hooks—Nos. 4 and 5. Another list of flies serviceable for the Loman has been supplied to me by an experienced angler in the district, and this consists of blue uprights, olive quill, and blue dun only. There are no fish in the Loman but trout. The stream, which is all private and preserved, flows for the most part through a clay soil; and in its upper parts it is well wooded and rather difficult to fish.

The Culm rises in the Black Downs, where are also situated the sources of the Otter and of one or two of the head branches of the Somerset- The Culm shire Tone, and flows to Culmstock through meadow and pasture lands bounded on either side by ridges and hills of the Black Downs. Below Culmstock it flows through a more open country,

passing Uffculme, Willand, and Cullompton, and
joining the Exe a little below Stoke Cannon.   Its
chief tributaries are the Kentisbere Brook of four
miles in length, the Ashford Brook of about the
same length, and the Longford Brook.   Trout are
numerous in the Culm, running commonly from
about seven ounces to one pound, and flies which may
be recommended are the blue upright, gold twist,
March brown, red palmer, silver twist, black gnat,
Culm spinner, Culm cinnamon—both dressed by
Mr. Austin of Tiverton—and May-fly.   The stream,
which is clear and rapid, and contains trout only,
is preserved from Cullompton to Kensham Mills
by the Culm Fishing Association, which begins the
season on February 15th—the Culm, like the Otter,
is an early water—and ends on August 31st.
Season tickets for this water are obtainable, and
strangers, provided they live fifteen miles off,
may get a monthly ticket.   At Culmstock, the
Culm Fishing Club has a portion of the stream up
to Hemyock.   Strangers can have daily tickets,
and the season begins on February 1st, and ends
on August 31st.   Tickets for these lengths are to
be had at the Railway Hotel, Culmstock, and the
Railway Hotel, Cullompton.

The Creedy is certainly one of the best trout
streams in Devonshire, and the fish run larger than

The   they do in most waters in the county.
Creedy   From its source near Puddington to within
about four miles of the spot where it joins the Exe
a little above St. David's, it is a fairly rapid river,
flowing through a hilly country, and swelled by
several lesser streams, such as the Sandford Brook,
the Fordton, the Yeo, and—below Crediton—by
the Shobrook.   From Crediton to Exeter is about

five miles. In many places the Creedy is much overgrown with alders and other bushes, and there is a good deal of barbed wire by its banks, which makes fishing somewhat difficult. There are no angling clubs or associations on this stream, which is strictly preserved by Mr. Quicke, General Sir Redvers Buller, V.C., Sir John Shelley, and Sir John Ferguson-Davie, who are the chief riparian owners. Trout are fairly plentiful, and run up to $1\frac{1}{2}$ lb. The March brown is a Creedy insect, and the blue upright, the half stone, and red palmer with peacock hackle are the usual Creedy angling flies ; whilst for evening fishing a coachman is useful.

The Rev. J. A. Welsh Collins, of Newton St. Cyres, on this stream, tells me he seldom changes his flies, commencing the season with blue upright March brown, and February red, or red palmer, and always keeping the first-named on his cast. A few dace find their way up the Creedy from the last few miles of the Exe, in which they are plentiful, but they are scarcely worth mentioning. Crediton (Ship Hotel) or Newton St. Cyres may be conveniently made headquarters by the angler.

The Teign rises in the centre of Dartmoor, and in its upper parts flows through some grand moor, rock, and woodland scenery. The **The Teign** lower Teign passes chiefly through a wide, fertile, and well-wooded valley. The angler may make his headquarters at Chagford (Moor Park, or Three Crowns) or Dunsford (Royal Oak), Newton Abbot (Globe) or Chudleigh (Clifford Arms). The two former are on the upper Teign, and the two latter on the lower Teign. The Upper Teign Association (Chagford) preserves six miles, and the Lower Teign Association (Newton

Abbot) preserves eight miles of the stream. Trout are plentiful in the upper water, running about four to the pound, with here and there a larger one ; they are less plentiful in the lower water, where, however, there are, I am told, "many sea trout and a few salmon." The Teign flies, as given me by an experienced angler, are the blue upright, March brown, iron blue dun, silver blue, hawthorn, and alder. The Upper Teign Association's trout season is from March 3rd to September 30th, and the same dates apply to the water of the Lower Teign Association. The stream has several small tributaries, such as the Wood Brook and Cherry Brook, with one large one, the Bovey.

The Bovey rises in the south-east of Dartmoor, flows for some miles in a north-east direction, **The** and then turns south-east, and, passing **Bovey** North Bovey and Bovey Tracey, joins the Teign about four miles above the estuary, which begins by Newton Abbot and extends to East Teignmouth. The stream is clear and rapid, flowing through some fine scenery. North Bovey is a pleasant place to stay at, and some trout fishing at a very moderate charge is to be obtained between this place and Bovey Tracey, five miles down stream. At Bovey Tracey there are two hotels, the Railway and the Dolphin ; and below the town the Lower Teign Fishing Association preserves the water. Wading is not allowed, and the minnow is prohibited till June 1st. The head-quarters of the Lower Teign Fishing Association are at Newton Abbot. Trout are pretty plentiful on the Bovey, and they occasionally run up to $1\frac{1}{2}$ lb. All the Teign flies are good for the Bovey,

together with the oak fly and red palmer. In
some parts of the stream worm fishing as well as
trolling is practised. There are salmon-peel in the
Bovey running from ½ lb. to 3 lbs.

The Dart. This beautiful trout stream rises in
two branches, called the East and the West Dart,
on Dartmoor. The latter, flowing through The
"Wistman's Wood," is joined at Two Dart
Bridges by the Cowsic, which "rushes down a
romantic ravine over the noblest masses of
granite broken into a thousand fantastic forms."
A little lower down the West Dart receives the
Blackabrook, which comes from Mis Tor, and flows
by that grim spot, Dartmoor Prison, and then the
Cherry Brook and the Swincombe. The two
branches of the Dart join by Dartmeet Bridge, and
the stream for some miles is then in private hands.
Above, the Dart and its tributaries can be fished
for a small payment by anglers staying at, among
other inns, the Duchy at Princetown, and the
Saracen's Head at Two Bridges. Before the Dart
reaches Ashburton, which is eleven miles below the
junction of the two branches, it receives the East
Webburn, four miles, and the West Webburn, seven
miles in length. The stream here flows through
deep ravines and richly wooded districts, and at
Buckland is the "Lovers' Leap," a mass of slate
rising sheer from the water—a fine bit of scenery.
By-and-by the Dart at Dartington flows through
some of the very best land in the county ; and here
the stream is comparatively placid. From Ashburton to Totnes is thirteen miles, and five miles
lower down the estuary is reached. Between Ashburton and the estuary, several tributaries flow into
the Dart, the largest one of twelve miles flowing

through Rattery and Harberton. The trout in the upper waters of the Dart and its tributaries run about five to the pound—some days the average will be as high as four to the pound ; in the lower waters the average varies between, four, three, and two to the pound, whilst now and then a fish of well over the pound is taken with fly, minnow, worm, maggot, or wasp-grub, which at times are all used. The artificial flies include the blue upright, red palmer, March brown, silver horns (brown), silver twist, stone fly, red upright, cowdung, Wickham fancy, and a pattern dressed with woodcock wing and hare's ear body. On the whole, the Dart is a clear and rapid stream—especially rapid in the moors— and it contains, besides trout, salmon-peel and eels.

It may be convenient at this point to give a list of the best and principal waters which can be fished by the Dartmoor angler, licenses being issued to the innkeepers and other agents by the Dart Conservators and the Tavy and Plym Board. These streams are the East and the West Dart, with the following tributaries :—the Blackabrook, the Cowsic, the Cherry Brook, and the Swincombe, the Plym with its tributaries, the Har Tor Brook, the Newlycombe Lake, and the Sheepstor Brook ; the Tavy with its tributaries, the Rattlebrook, the Bagga Tor Brook, the Willsworthy Brook, the Petertavy Brook, and the Wallcombe ; the Yealm ; the Erme ; the Lyd ; the Avon. The East and West Okement streams and the Taw are dealt with separately later on. Princetown, which many anglers make their Dartmoor headquarters, is very well situated for the East and the West Dart, and the East and the West Plym.

The Dartmoor streams

The Erme, a clear and rapid stream, but peat coloured in flood time, is among the half-hundred waters that take their rise on Dartmoor. **The Erme** It is about sixteen miles in length, and has three small tributaries, the Ugborough Brook (which receives the little Wood Brook), the Shilstone Brook, and the Modbury Brook. The trout of the Erme and its tributaries run small— about six to the pound—but they are plentiful. Fly fishing is the method of fishing up to June 1st, after which date the minnow and the worm are allowed by the Avon and Erme Fishery Association. The flies for the Erme are the stone fly, March brown, coch-a-bonddu, red and black palmers, red upright, blue uprights, alder, and black gnat. The Erme holds no other fish besides trout. Ivybridge is the best place for the angler to make his headquarters at, and tickets may there be obtained for the water. For six miles the Erme flows through the moorland, and from Dartmoor to the sea it is a well-wooded stream. Fleet House, the beautiful seat of the Mildmay family, is on this stream.

The Yealm, a stream of some seventeen miles in length, rises on Dartmoor, and passes Cornwood Yealmton, and Newton Ferrers. The **The Yealm** Yealm, which sometimes runs very low in a dry summer, receives several small tributaries, the Braxton Water, five miles in length, being the most considerable, and the tide flows up to within about a mile of Yealmton. The Yealm has no angling club, and is preserved in its fishing length by private owners and occupiers. It is thickly wooded throughout almost its entire length, with the exception of half a mile or so above Cornwood, where it takes its rise in the open moor, and it is a clear and rapid stream. On Dartmoor, and for two miles below, trout are plentiful but very small. Lower down the Yealm the fish run up to ½ lb., and a 1½-lb. fish has been taken. The best artificial flies are thought by local anglers of experience to be the blue upright, the half stone, the coch-a-bonddu, and the infallible. On the upper parts of the Yealm the artificial fly is commonly used, but near the estuary the Devon minnow is preferred by most anglers. The Yealm has during the summer months a good number of salmon-peel.

The Avon is a stream of about eight-and-twenty miles in length, which rises on Dartmoor, and flows by **The Avon** Brent, Diptford, Loddiswell, and Aveton Gifford, up to which place the tide flows. It receives some small tributaries, the largest of which is the Woodleigh Brook, which flows in a few miles above the estuary. Brent is the best place for the angler to make his headquarters at on the upper portion of the stream, and by a small daily payment the lower waters may be fished from Newhouse or Loddiswell where there is accommodation. Trout are fairly plentiful, though they run somewhat small, and the best flies are perhaps the blue upright; the coch-a-bonddu is also used.

The Tamar, says Skrine, "abounds in fine features and majestic outline." Rising in the parish **The Tamar** of Moorwenstowe, in the extreme northern corner of Cornwall, it flows in a southeast direction to the English Channel at Plymouth, passing through much beautiful scenery, and separating for many miles the counties of Devonshire and Cornwall. Its watershed is largely under

cultivation, and the land on its banks is chiefly
devoted to pasture, though there is a certain
amount used for arable purposes, while here and
there there are some copses and plantations. It
has a number of tributaries, chief among which
are—on the Devonshire side—the Deer, the Carey,
the Lyd, with its tributaries the Lew and Thistle
Brook, and the Tavy, which is separately described.
The stream flows by North Tamerton (Cornwall),
Boyton (Cornwall), and by Lifton (Devon), and
Launceston (Cornwall), and by New Bridge, Calstock (Cornwall), a little below which place the tide
is reached. Launceston or Lifton—the two places
are opposite one another on different sides of the
river—makes about the best angling headquarters
for the angler who intends fishing the upper part
of the Tamar or its tributaries north of Tavistock.
There are several hotels and inns at Launceston,
among them the King's Arms and the White
Hart, and it is usually possible for a stranger
to get permission for a few days for the Tamar
here, or for its Devon or Cornwall tributaries.
Launceston and Tavistock are connected by a
branch of the Great Western Railway, which en-
ables the angler to get pretty easily, through the
stations at Lidford, Coryton, and Lifton, at the
Lid, Lew, Thistle Brook, and other tributaries of
the Tamar. The Tamar cannot, I think, be described as a very clear and rapid stream. From its
source to Launceston it runs through a clay, rather
than rock-bound country, and the pools are long—
sometimes upwards of a quarter of a mile. Lower
down, however, the Tamar is considerably cleared
by several more streams, notably by the Lyd.
Trout are plentiful in the upper portions of the

Tamar, as well as in most of the tributaries, but they run small. A basket of, say, five dozen fish, weighing about 15 lbs., would be regarded as one of the best of the season, though I am told that trout up to 1½ lbs., and even 2 lbs., have been occasionally taken, especially in the stretches of the Tamar below Launceston. A correspondent writes to me—"Years ago, when I was young, fish in the beautiful Tamar were plentiful"—he is speaking of the lower water—" and they were then often called the glittering or golden trout, owing to the bright marks on their backs, which shone out most distinctly when they were 'grid-ironed'—the Cornish method of cooking them." Another correspondent compares the Tamar, in regard both to the country through which it flows and its trout, to the River Watach in the Black Forest.

Fly fishing is general on the Tamar and its upper tributaries, and the artificials recommended are the February red, March brown, grannam, hawthorn, palmers, Maxwell blue, and blue and silver. Salmon and salmon-peel were formerly always found in the stream in the winter months, but their numbers seem to have much diminished. They come up too late for angling purposes. Dace are plentiful in the Tamar.

Turner was well acquainted with some of the finest scenery on the Tamar, which he painted in his *Crossing the Brook*. The river drains one of the largest areas of any river flowing into the English Channel—namely, 600 square miles. The Exe drains an area of 645, and the (Christchurch) Avon an area of 673 square miles.

The Tavy, which contains some salmon-peel and salmon, in addition to trout, rises at Cranmere

Pool, near the source of the Dart on Dartmoor, a few miles from Lidford. It receives, before it joins the Tamar, the Rattle Brook, the Woolmer, The the Wallcombe, the Bagga Tor Brook, Tavy the Willsworthy Brook, and the Petertavy Brook. The Tavy passes Tavistock and Walreddon, where the steep hills and masses of wood above the stream form some fine scenery. This river is clearer than the Tamar, and it flows rapidly, so that the poet Browne wrote of " Tavie's voyceful stream." At Tavy Cleave, Mary-Tavy and Peter-Tavy the stream flows through a rugged and desolate country, and at the former place it is full of sound and fury in floodtime as it roars beneath its masses of overhanging crag. Tickets to fish the Tavy are issued by the Tavy and Plym Association, a shilling for the day or a sovereign for the season. The trout run about the same size as those of the Tamar, and they are supposed to be less bright in colour; they rarely come down into the brackish water. The flies recommended for the Tamar may be used for the Tavy.

The Torridge, a river of some 60 miles from source to sea, rises near the sea at Barnstaple Bay, and not far from the source of the Tamar. Owing to The the peaty moors through which it travels in Torridge its upper portions, the stream is of a brownish colour. The Torridge comes from near Hartland, and soon receives some tributary streams, amongst them being the Waldon. The course of the river is somewhat eccentric. Between its source and Black Torrington, it flows south-east; then for some miles to the point where the Lew joins, it flows due east; and, finally, turning sharply round, makes for Barnstaple and Bideford Bay, flowing

M

towards the north-west. By river Bideford is 60 miles from the Ditchen Hills, where the Torridge takes its rise; as the crow flies, the distance between the two places is scarcely more than a dozen miles, and Bideford is actually the nearest station to the source of the stream and the upper portion of the tributary, called the Seckington Water. How numerous are the tributaries which swell the Torridge may be gathered from the following list, which by no means includes all the lesser waters or the tributaries of tributaries:— The Seckington Water, Floodmead Water, Waldon, Whiteleigh Brook, Buckland Brook, Lew (which has several feeders), Okement (which has the East Okement), Exbourne Water, Merton Brook, Waley Brook, Langtree Brook, Hunshaw Water, Laidland Water, and Wear Water. Of these the Waldon, the Lew and Okement are the largest, and the last-named may be said to connect the Torridge with Dartmoor. The Okement and the Taw are the two streams which carry Dartmoor water to Barnstaple Bay. All the other streams take the Dartmoor water to the English Channel, through the Exe, Dart, Tamar, Teign, and other lesser rivers. The Torridge is, except at one or two points, such as Great Torrington, a somewhat difficult stream for the angler to reach, as it is not situated in a land of railway stations. Great Torrington, however, is pretty easily reached by Barnstaple, and the Globe inn preserves eight miles of the stream for its visitors. Again there is fishing to be obtained by anglers staying at the Half Moon at Sheepwash, which is situated at about the middle of the Torridge, and can be reached from either Hollacombe or Holsworthy station.

On the whole, trout are plentiful in the Torridge, small in the upper portion, but lower down, in the neighbourhood of Great Torrington, a good basket may be expected to contain fish from ¼ lb. to 1 lb. The minnow is very often used from June to August, but earlier in the season wet fly fishing is general, and the flies in favour are, amongst others, the blue upright, March brown, and red palmer. The Torridge contains salmon-peel, and some dace in its lower portions. It is a rapid stream, passing through some beautiful scenery, and its course is entirely, I believe, within the altered carboniferous rocks of Devonshire.

The Waldon rises in the neighbourhood of Bradworthy and, passing Sutcombe and Thornbury, joins the Torridge about three miles above Black Torrington. In its upper stretches it runs through a boggy moor, and is more wooded just before it joins the Torridge. The Waldon is clear and fast, and in the winter, when the stream is full, a few salmon-peel occasionally find their way some distance up it. There are plenty of trout averaging about four or five to the pound, and the blue upright is considered the best artificial fly. Worm and minnow are used as well as fly. Holsworthy is the nearest station to the Waldon, and is about five miles distant.

The Okement proper, or West Okement, rises on Dartmoor by Cranmere Pool, and close to where the Tavy, the Dart, and the Taw have their head waters. From its source to Okehampton the Okement runs about nine or ten miles through the moor, and some eight miles below Okehampton it unites with the Torridge. The East Okement rises in a bog called Skit

M 2

Bottom, on Dartmoor, and, after a course of five miles or so, joins the West Okement just below Okehampton. The higher waters of the Okement are now very little fished, owing to the Artillery practice on Dartmoor, which is dangerous except to those who happen to know exactly at what range the shooting is being carried on. Below the town the Okement is much wooded, and it is necessary to wade—and to wade carefully, as the stream is inclined to be treacherous. Fish are very plentiful on the moor above Okehampton, but small, running from ten to twelve to the pound. Baskets of from four to eight dozen of these troutlets are made by good anglers when the water is more or less copper-coloured. Below Okehampton the average is about five to the pound, and trout of 1 lb. and of over 2 lbs. have occasionally been taken in this water. There is no better fly than a blue upright the season through, and when the water is coloured, a fly with plenty of tinsel, gold or silver twist, is often found killing. Some of the local anglers fish with worm, and in the evenings with cheese! The stream is ordinarily very clear and rapid, with rocky pools here and there. Between Okehampton and the Torridge the Okement flows through meadow land. Tickets for angling in the stream can be obtained from the White Hart Hotel in the town.

The Taw has its source at Tawhead on Dartmoor, and flows north-east for about the first half **The Taw** of its course, when it turns north-west, and flows in that direction to Barnstaple Bay. It flows by Belston, on the edge of Dartmoor, South Tawton, North Tawton, Eggesford, South Molton Road Station, Umberleigh, and Bishop's

Tawton, two miles below which place it enters upon
its estuary at Barnstaple. Its three chief tributaries are the Lapford Water, with its tributary the
Washford Brook, Little Dart—which flows in near
Chumleigh—the Yeo, with its tributaries the Mole
and the Bray, and the Kentisbury Water, which
flows in at Barnstaple. There is a fair head of
trout in the upper portions of the Taw, where
they run about a quarter of a pound apiece. The
artificial fly is principally used before the beginning of May, after which time the minnow is
the favourite lure on this stream. The flies chiefly
used are the blue uprights, March brown, iron
blue dun, yellow dun, olive and blue dun, red
spinner, red (and silver) palmer, and half stone.
Salmon are found in the lower portions of the
Taw after the first high flood of October, and,
if the summer be sufficiently wet, a fair number
of fish ascend again in July. Salmon-peel, which
fifteen years ago were usually abundant in July,
have now, by reason of over-netting in the estuary,
become exceedingly scarce. There are no angling
clubs or associations on the Taw, but strangers
staying at the Fox and Hounds, Eggesford, or at
the Fortescue Arms, South Molton Road Station,
can get fishing.

The Little Dart, which receives the Sturcombe
above Witheridge, is one of the chief tributaries of
the Taw. It rises on Rackenford Moor, **The**
and joins the main river a little below **Little**
Eggesford station. The Little Dart flows **Dart**
through a hilly and very pretty country, and
contains a good number of trout, running from
three ounces to half a pound, whilst occasionally
one may take a 1-lb. fish. In summer the Little

Dart, which contains some salmon-peel, dace, and,
I believe, a few perch, often runs low, and the best
fly fishing is over by May. The flies for this
stream are the blue uprights, March brown, and
rusty reds and blues. There are no angling clubs
on the Little Dart, and season tickets for eight
miles of the water may be obtained at the Fox
and Hounds at Eggesford. The fishing is free for
those who stay at the hotel.

The Yeo is a considerable stream, joining the Taw
just below South Molton Road Station. Several
The of its branches rise in the high ridges
Yeo which form the outskirts of Exmoor, and
they all contain plenty of trout, some of which
run up to half a pound. The streams, which include besides the Yeo, the Mole, the Bray, and the
Molland Water, are clear and rapid, and fly fishing
is the almost invariable method of angling practised. The blue uprights, March brown, and
february red are used at the commencement of the
season, and later on the black gnat, red spinner,
and May-fly, with the coachman and white moth
for evening fishing. South Molton is the best place
perhaps for the angler to make his headquarters at,
and the George Hotel there has several miles of
fishing. Lord Poltimore preserves water on both
the Bray and Mole, and often gives leave to fish.
There are sometimes a few salmon and peel in the
lower waters of the Yeo, near its junction with the
Taw. Both Yeo and Mole have their origin in and
flow through rocks of the Devonian period.

II. CORNWALL

The Inney, a tributary of the Tamar, which it joins a few miles below Dunterton, rises by Davidstown and flows by St. Clether, **The** Lancast, and Lewannick. It is among **Inney** the best trouting waters of Cornwall, and its fish are earlier and better fed than those of the neighbouring Lynher. It is preserved by Mr. C. G. Archer of Trelaske, Launceston, who occasionally grants permission to fly fishermen and others, and trout of the usual Tamar size are plentiful. The Inney and its tributary the Penpont Water may be fished with the flies recommended for the Tamar, and Launceston makes the best headquarters. The Ottery and the Attery, two other Cornwall branches of the Tamar, are also within fairly easy reach of Launceston. Further north, in the corner of the county, there is a little trouting in the Bude and its branches—which are reached from Holsworthy railway station in Devonshire—as well as in the Bude and Launceston Canal reservoir.

The Lynher rises near Fox Tor, north-west of Bodmin Moor, and, flowing south-east almost throughout its course, joins the Tamar **The** estuary at Saltash. It passes through **Lynher** densely wooded country of slate and granite hills. The Cascade river, which is strictly preserved by Mr. Rodd of Trebartha Hall, Launceston, flows through tamer scenery. The Lynher trout are decidedly late for Cornwall, which is perhaps the earliest angling county in the South, and are not in condition much before the middle of April. They are plentiful, and run about eight to the pound. Fly fishing is the only method of angling practised, and the artificials include the blue uprights, red palmer, coch-a-bonddu, &c. Nearly the whole of the upper portion of the Lynher is in the hands of Mr. Rodd, who is generous in granting permission to many fly fishermen. The water three miles below Trebartha Hall is poisoned by the Phœnix Mine, and no fish are found from that point to the estuary. Salmon and peel used to ascend the stream, but not one has been seen for the last forty or fifty years, though the remains of salmon hatches are still in existence, as well as the lease of the old Trebartha Mill, with its weir and salmon hatch. The water is strictly preserved by the owner of Trebartha Hall, and is about a six or seven miles' drive from Launceston, the nearest railway station.

The Camel takes its rise between Boscastle and Camelford, and flows south-west to a point close to **The Camel** Bodmin, where it turns round and flows north-west, to empty itself into the sea at Padstow Bay. It is navigable for eight miles from the sea, and receives the following streams and brooks:—the Gaspard, De Lank, Bisland Water, Lanivet Water, Withiel Water, Kestle Water, and Combe Water. Besides these streams, the Camel is fed by very many rivulets coming from the wild moors of East Cornwall. On or near the banks of the Camel are Camelford (King's Avon Hotel), which may be made headquarters, if the angler is fishing the upper part of the stream ; Michaelstow ; St. Tudy, which lies midway between the Camel and its chief tributary the Kettle ; Bodmin; and Wadebridge, where the estuary begins. A Cornwall angler writes to me concerning the Camel and its district :—" If the fishing is confined

to the Camel, St. Breward probably makes the
best centre, though Camelford is regarded as a
good spot for the angler, because it commands
several other waters. The Devil's Jump Stream,
which rises near Roughton, and joins the Camel at
the Devil's Jump about two miles from Camelford,
is a good water, and open till near the point where
it unites with the main stream, where it becomes
wooded, and fly fishing is difficult. The Valency
river is also a good trout water. It is five
miles from Camelford, and, rising between
Lesnewth and Otterham stations, joins the sea at
Boscastle."

Trout are decidedly plentiful on the Camel and
its tributaries, and seven dozen or over have been
taken by an angler in an afternoon. A considerable number run up to about ½ lb. ; a few
are taken of 1 lb. ; whilst about the largest on record seems to be one of 2 lbs. The artificial flies
chiefly used include the blue uprights, red palmer
yellow dun, blue dun, willow fly, alder, coch-
a-bonddu, red spinner, and the coachman for
evening fishing. There are no angling clubs or
associations on the Camel, and it is often possible
to get permission for a day or two's angling in the
main stream, or in the tributaries, some of which
flow through remote districts where heather, stunted
grass, and the whortleberry form almost the sole
vegetation. The lower parts of the Camel are
chiefly wooded. Some salmon and salmon-peel
come up the Camel, and are to be taken at times
with the fly.

The Fowey rises near Brown Willy and, flowing
south by Bodmin Moor, runs for some miles
parallel with the Great Western Railway between

Liskeard and Lostwithiel. The Fowey has some fair trouting above Red Gate, and below Lord **The** Robartes gives leave between Lostwithiel **Fowey** and Glynn, which portions of the stream are well wooded. Minnow is used as well as fly, and September is sometimes a good month for this stream and its tributaries which rise in Bodmin Moor. Red and black palmers, blue uprights, blue dun, March brown, and coch-a-bonddu are useful flies here, as indeed on most other Cornwall streams. Liskeard should be made headquarters for the upper parts of the Fowey, from which town the St. Germans stream—a tributary of the Lynher—and the Looe and West Looe, which flow into Looe Bay at the small town bearing that name, may also be easily reached. The hotel at Liskeard is Webb's.

The Camel, Lynher, Inney, Ottery, and Fowey may be regarded as the five chief streams of Cornwall; but there are many others, chief among them the Hel and the beautiful Fal, containing plenty of troutlets and some salmon-peel as well. The Loe Pool, near Helston, was once celebrated for its excellent trout, and there is a story of one weighing no less than 8 lbs. 3 oz., taken there with fly in 1774 ! It is now not the water it used to be, owing to tin mine poisoning ; but there are troutlets in the Cober hard by, and in dozens of other nameless little streams in this part of Cornwall. The Cornwall troutlets are frequently in condition by February, and the flies recommended for the Fowey will be found to be of general use.

APPENDIX

[Mr. E. Goble, of Fareham, has kindly allowed me to make use of the following quaint notes concerning the Arle, compiled some thirty years or so since by a keen old angler, who, sad to relate, ended his life in a Hampshire workhouse.]   **The Arle**

"Fifty years' observations of the fishes now and here-before inhabiting the New River, as it was and is called, at Titchfield from the Flood Hatches (where it empties into the sea) up to the flour mill at Titchfield, showing the different sorts of food they live on and many other particulars which, it is presumed, are unknown to the gentlemen comprising the Fishing Club, and also as regards the river named the Old, nearly as far as Funtley flour mill downwards to the New Bridge at the lower part of the Haven near Hill Head. It may be as well to observe that the author of these and the following lines had annually stake nets during the above period for thirty years for the purpose of catching fishes contained in Southampton Water, shifting them from time to time from the latter end of February until the latter end of August, when he used to take them up until the next year.

"The reader will be kind enough to excuse the manner in which these lines are written, as the author apparently digresses from the subject, but as long as he makes himself clearly understood, that he deems sufficient for the purpose he aims at. Both rivers contain salmon, salmon-peel,[1] trouts, eels, grey mullet, bass (the two last

---

[1] Called salmon when their weight is 10 lbs.; under that, salmon-peel, or, as some call them, salmon-smelts.

named were to be chiefly found in the Old River),
flounders of all sizes up to 3 and 4 lbs. each, minnows,
lampreys and cray-fish.   Salmon and salmon-peel enter
both rivers every month in the year, and there remain,
if not caught, until their spawning time.   The author
has known some of them spawn when the water has been
thick, as early as the middle of October.   These are
termed by him forward fish.   Some stop until November
and December, and as late as the latter end of February.
The earlier they spawn the earlier they are in season the
next spring.   Those that spawn in October are as good
the next March as those which spawn in December are
in May, and so on.   After they have spawned they
return to the sea, and where they roam to and how far I
know not ; but this I know, that they return to the same
spot, or nearly so, when their spawning time comes again.
Now it is said that a salmon-peel of a pound weight will,
in the space of twelve months become of 6 lbs.   This I
doubt much by reason of the following experiments.   In
the month of November, I caught twelve salmon-peel of
about 1 lb. each.   I took six of them and cut off one
half the tail of each.   I put a piece of copper wire about
the size of a small ring through the nose of each of the
other six, and turned them adrift in the water I had
taken them from.   In the following November I went
to see if they were there, and found two whose tails were
cut, and three with the rings in their noses.   As near as
I could judge they did not each weigh more than 2¼ lbs.
This is proof also of what I have stated about the fish
returning to the same spots.   It may be asked, Why
were not the twelve that were put in there?   The
answer is that they might have been preyed upon
by other fish, or have been caught, or have died.   I
can say nought about other rivers in this country or
elsewhere : I form my opinion from the Titchfield
rivers.

"Salmon and salmon-peel will rise at artificial flies in the
spring and during the summer months.   I never myself
caught any in this manner, but before Hammonds Bridge,
as far as the Flood Hatches, have seen gentlemen catch
them of the weight of 6 and 7 lbs., and no larger.   One
of these gentlemen said he had twice caught a larger

salmon. Iron Mill Pond extends from the mill nearly
up to Funtley flour mill, and in the little river called the
back river, which goes as far as Long Water Bridge
hatches, salmon-peel from 1 lb. to 5 and 6 lbs. have been
caught. In the month of February, should the weather be
mild, which some years it is, good sport can be had fishing
with an artificial palmer fly, taking some trout from 1 to
2 lbs., as well as salmon-peel from ½ to 2 lbs., with a breeze
from the south-west to cause a ripple on the water. In
the small river named above, salmon and salmon-peel
spawn from just below the iron mills on different beds
of gravel, and opposite to them, and also in the little
back river as far as Long Water Bridge. There are
lampreys in the rivers all the way, and they spawn in
the beds of gravel used by the salmon and salmon-peel,
commencing in April.

"Many persons labour under a great mistake concerning
salmon at their spawning time. The male is of a red
colour, with a hook in its lower jaw, which rises above
its upper jaw, and they fancy it is a different species of
fish, and call it the trout bouger. The hook in the jaw
is caused by its being poor. That there has been fish
in Southampton Water with large red spots on them, as
have river trout, I know, for one year I caught them in
my nets from 1 lb. up to 7 and 8 lbs., but no larger, as many
as sixteen in one week. They were the same year caught
in the Haven, and up the Old River. Their flesh was
of a bright red colour, and gentlemen who purchased
them said they were most delicious, preferable to salmon.
They left suddenly, and I never saw any of the kind
afterwards.

"Salmon and salmon-peel are very silly fishes, for when
they enter the river, and a person happens to espy them
as they are swimming along, they will make for the first
hollow under a bank, and should they be unable to hide
their whole bodies within it, so long as their head is out
of sight, they will allow themselves to be thrown out of
the water. This is so with regard to trout also.

"A mullet can swim fast. I have seen in the summer
large salmon-peel swimming along with roaches, and
now and then the salmon-peel would dart at and catch
a roach of ½ lb. or so, in the same manner as a trout will

at a minnow. The roaches take not the least notice of
the loss of one of their companions, neither do the
minnows. Trouts feed in the winter on little fresh-water
winkles. A large quantity of eels are caught by "quad-
ding" a corruption of the proper word "bobbing," and
the method is as follows :—A person provides himself
with a stiff ashen pole of the length of 10 feet, with a
line attached to it, which must be very strong, as large
(say) as horse net twine. This line has at the end of it
a leaden plummet of 6 ounces in weight. A quantity of
earth-worms are put on double thread with a piece of
small wire and wound round the hand backwards and
forwards and tied to the line just below the plummet.
The angler then sounds the bottom, and keeps the worms
about 1 inch from it, and when an eel bites the angler
pulls up and throws the eel out of the river. Should the
water be thick after rain, the angler tries for them at all
times of the day, and has been known to catch 40 and
sometimes 60 lbs. weight in a day. This has been
practised from time immemorial without any person
being forbidden. Eels, when the water is clear and the
weather is very hot, will bite in the day time, if the angler
tries among weeds or sedge. If they do not bite then,
he waits until the evening, and if they do not come on
about 9 o'clock, it is of no use. Sometimes they will
not bite even in what is considered good weather for two
or three days. It is of no use whatever to try of a
bright moonlight night, for, although they will bite as
fast as possible, not one is caught. The instant it is
attempted to pull them out they let go the worm as they
reach the top of the water. This happens when the
water is clear, but it is not so when it is thick. When a
eel bites it is obliged to turn round with its belly upwards,
and spins round and round to get the worms off. A
shark acts in the same manner. Eels are found in most
rivers and ponds. In rivers, when the spring commences,
they swim against the stream, let it be ever so swift, and
will jump over hatches as well as salmon. I have seen
them do so. Provided the water that runs over the
hatches is in bulk no larger than that which runs off the
nose of a common pump, they will succeed most
assuredly."

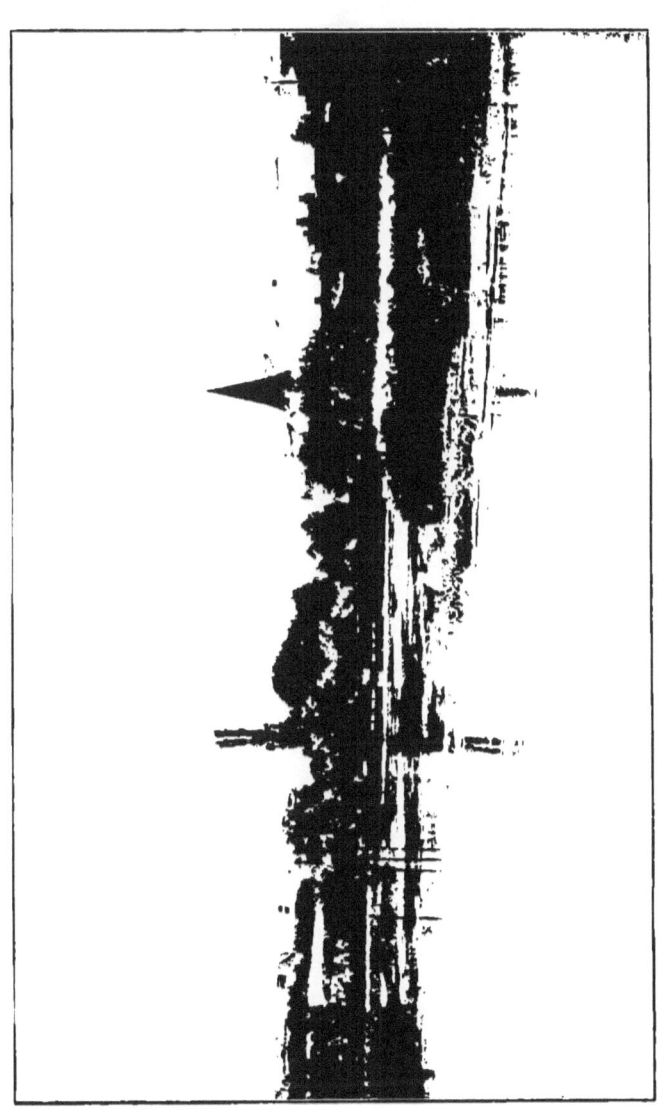

THE TEST AT STOCKBRIDGE.

Some interesting notes concerning this pretty and little-known tributary of the Anton appeared in Major Turle's " Reminiscences of an Angler " in the *Fishing*   The
Gazette in January, 1893. He described the   Pillhill
Pillhill as being nearly as long as the Anton   Brook
itself, but much less in size.   " It was but a poor little
stream until the Marquess of Winchester undertook the
regeneration of it where it flows through his property at
Amport, and, by dint of digging, delving, damming,
creating artificial falls, widening, and improving in every
way, made insignificant Pill Brook into a fishable stream
containing trout upwards of a pound in weight. It is worth
the while of any one contemplating the formation of a
trout stream to pay Pill Brook a visit at Amport in order
to see what can be done for a mere rivulet by means of
patience, perseverance, and . . . . money." A stretch
of this little stream is in the hands of Mr. Henry
Hammans, of Clatford Lodge, who some years ago stocked
it with trout.   Unfortunately the fish were killed through
a horrible volume of mud which was allowed to come
down from above.   There are, however, still some fish in
Mr. Hammans's grounds, and there is a pond which
Mr. Francis Francis many years ago caused to be made
with the idea of trying to hatch and rear trout there.   It
is altogether a charming spot, of which I shall never
entertain any but agreeable memories.

Some fair bags have been made from time to time on
the Pillhill. A friend wrote to me in 1896, telling me he
had killed in eight days thirty-five trout, weighing 30 lbs.

Jesse, that delightful naturalist and writer on country
life, angled occasionally in the Test, and has something
to say of the difficulty of hooking trout in the   The Test
stream.   So far back as 1836 he found that he
could not take trout with an artificial fly in bright sun-
shine—though these were the days when Colonel Hawker,
higher up stream, was doing so well—and he was driven
to try the blowline and a natural fly.   "At particular
seasons," he declares, " it requires a master of the rod to
have a chance of taking any good-sized fish, and, speaking generally, a bungler had better try his luck in any
other stream."   He recommended four artificial flies for

the Test—a small light-coloured one and a small dark-coloured one for use when the water was clear and still, and two large ones of the same shades for morning and evening fishing, when there was "a good curl on the water, or a strong stream."

At one time the Leckford was the leading club, it would seem, on the Test. Richard Brinsley Sheridan, if not a member of the club, was to be seen there; whilst Tom Sheridan (who had the unenviable reputation of taking undersized fish sometimes) was a member and a regular frequenter. Very gay and frolicsome must gatherings of the members often have been, and one at least of their rules points to a good deal of chaff and fun. This rule read thus—"No drawing, painting, sketch, or model of any trout shall be taken at the general expense, unless such a fish shall have exceeded 5 lbs., and shall have been *bona fide* caught by one of the party, and not privately bought at Stockbridge." By another rule a fine of ten and sixpence was imposed on "any member who described the strength, size, &c., of any immense fish which had just got off at the point of being landed."

In his interesting and instructive book on *Water and Water Supply* (Messrs. W. H. Allen & Co.) Mr. Ansted gives an excellent general description of what **"Water** he calls the "drainage area of the south of Eng-**and** land," from which I take the liberty of making **Water** **Supply."** the following quotation, though the whole book should be studied by those who wish to thoroughly understand our river system :—

" 1. *General Account of the District.*—The country here understood as the south of England consists of two parts : One is the long narrow strip south of the Thames basin, extending from the South Foreland at Dover westwards for nearly 150 miles to the Isle of Portland, very narrow at the eastern extremity, but widening towards the west to about 40 miles. This forms the eastern district beyond it, and still more to the west there remains the promontory of Cornwall Devon, reaching for nearly 180 miles further in the same direction. The breadth of this latter part, at first about 60 miles, gradually narrows to

little more than 10 at the extreme west. The whole area
may be roughly estimated to contain about 8,000 square
miles, and it includes the whole or parts of the following
counties : Kent, Sussex, Hampshire, Wiltshire, Dorset
shire, Somersetshire, Devonshire, and Cornwall. The
country in the eastern division rises rather rapidly to about
640 feet,[1] but nowhere attains any considerable elevation.
It drains almost everywhere towards the south. The
western district rises in Dartmoor to nearly 1,800 feet.
Beyond Dorsetshire the promontory, including Cornwall
and Devonshire, no longer drains entirely to the south,
but has an irregular line of water-parting connecting a
succession of granitic bases and throwing off the water
chiefly to the south but partly to the north. The whole
district is without any large river. The waters that fall
on the surface run quickly into the sea by a number of
streams from about forty catchments, but the lines of
watershed that part them only rise in a few places much
above the general level. The climate of the whole tract
is greatly influenced by its position with regard to the
English Channel and the Atlantic Ocean. It is everywhere mild and inclined to be damp, but this is chiefly
recognised in the south-western part where the atmos-
phere is generally near the point of saturation.

"2. *Condition of the Surface and Geological Structure.*
—The south downs, consisting of chalk hills, which
present a steep face to the sea for a long distance, termi-
nating at Beachy Head, form the characteristic feature of
the south-east of England. They are flat-topped, the
chalk is very near the surface, and being an absorbent
rock the rain that falls rapidly disappears. At intervals
the line is interrupted by depressions admitting of the
passage of rivers by which the surface is drained, and, as
is very generally the case in the chalk districts, the rivers
intersect the strike of the chalk about at right angles.
Eastwards from Beachy Head to Folkestone the country
is low and flat, and consists of rocks underlying the chalk,

Combe Hill in the extreme N.W. of Hampshire is as high as
936 feet. Doles Woods, formerly the home of the author of
The South Country Trout Streams, rise to 636 feet, whilst Colling-
bourne Woods, a few miles off, can show a height of 648 feet. All
are chalk hills.

N

but covered with alluvium. Advancing westwards into
Dorsetshire the oolites appear, but they occupy only a
small breadth of country. From the Isle of Purbeck,
where the upper wealden beds are found, to Portland
Island, where the upper oolites are developed and yield
a valuable building stone, the distance is very small, and
from Portland Bill to Lyme Regis, where the lias comes up
from beneath the oolites, it is also inconsiderable. The
new red sandstone, which then succeeds, is of greater
breadth, but by far the most completely developed deposits
are those still further to the west and much older, belonging to the Devonian period, the intervening carboniferous
series being abundantly but not characteristically represented. Granite bases have brought up these rocks and
the surface has been subsequently denuded. It is only
in the northern parts of Devonshire and in parts of Cornwall that the slates and shales of these ancient periods
come to the surface ; but there they entirely replace the
more modern deposits. The nature of the rocks has a
marked influence on the quantity as well as the quality
of the waters that run off the surface, as the physical condition of the surface and its orography influence the
quantity of rain that falls in the district.

" 3. *Sub-division of the District.*—The whole district
naturally divides into two. The eastern portion extends
from the South Foreland to the western watershed of the
Hampshire and Wiltshire Avon, and includes the country
south of the Thames basin. This part is the smallest,
has the fewer streams, and the smaller rainfall, with the
exception of the drainage area of the Stour, which is the
western branch of the Avon ; the rivers are all short,
commencing only a few miles back from the sea. The
western portion of this extensive district has a much
larger surface, many more streams, higher elevation, and
a heavier rainfall ; but the streams are scarcely more
important, and none of them possess more than local
interest. The western group of streams is again sub-
divided into two, those which drain southwards to the
English Channel, and those which empty themselves into
the Bristol Channel flowing towards the north.

" 4. *Sources of Water Supply.*--The eastern rivers of
this district have their sources in the wealden rocks, or

chalk, or the rock immediately underlying the one or overlying the other. Those that rise in the lower cretaceous or wealden deposits, break through the line of chalk hills and cross a considerable distance of chalk. Those, on the contrary, that rise on the ocean deposits, hardly leave them till they reach the sea. Advancing westwards where the oolites and lias are crossed, and the new red sandstone entered, we find a few streams of no great importance running over those rocks, especially in the eastern part of Devonshire. After this we enter the region of igneous and metamorphic rocks, and the drainage, whether to south or north, runs almost entirely over material little permeable, and not likely to retain, even for a short time, any considerable part of the fall. The flow of the streams here is large compared with the rainfall, but on the whole inconsiderable for want of breadth in country crossed. The country rises to a considerable elevation in Cornwall and Devonshire, and the sources of the rivers, whether from springs or surface drainage, are often very abundantly supplied. The rainfall being frequent they rarely fail, and are not often lowered for a long period of time.

"5. *Rainfall.*—The rainfall over the western part of the district is heavy, and the number of rainy days very considerable; but advancing eastward the quantity of rain sensibly diminishes, and the distribution is also greatly modified. In some parts of Cornwall the fall amounts to 47 inches; but even in that county exposed to warm moist winds blowing from the Atlantic, there are spots where it is said not to exceed 22 inches. The average of the district is taken at 36 inches. In Devonshire, or Dartmoor, the fall exceeds 52 inches; but at Sidmouth is said not to exceed 16½. The fall is very great on the high ground in the middle of the country; but in the sheltered nooks on the coast looking towards the east is everywhere comparatively small. In Somersetshire the fall is only 19 inches at Taunton, but increases towards the west and north. In Dorsetshire it ranges from 18½ at Abbotsbury to 29 at Blanford. In Hampshire it appears to be considerable, and towards western Sussex is found to amount to 34, while in parts of eastern Sussex it appears to be 33. At Hastings, though still consider-

able, the fall is 29 inches.   It will be evident from these
figures that the rainfall over the district is moderately
heavy, but is very dependent on local conditions.   On
the whole, here as elsewhere, the amount diminishes towards the east, and is greatest on high ground ; but
there are many apparent exceptions.

"6. *Quality of Waters.*—Flowing generally over favour-
able soils through agricultural districts not thickly peopled,
and over tracts of country not much cultivated, the waters
of the south of England, from whatever source, are
generally good.   The rivers coming over the granite of
Cornwall and the granitic and metamorphic rocks of
North Devon carry excellent water, and the chalk waters
of the eastern district are also excellent."

INDEX

Braemore, Avon (Christchurch) at, 125
Bransbury Common, Test at, 100, 103
Test tributary at, 100
Braughing, Quin above, 74
Bray, the, 166
Brede, the, 67
Brendon, Lyn at, 141
Brent, Avon (Devon) at, 158
Bridges, Colonel—on Test, 106
Bridges, Mr. J. H.—a Wandle proprietor, 58
Bridport, Asker at, 121
Bristol, Frome at, 87
Bristol Waterworks Company on Chew Magna, 139
Britt, the, 120
Broad Chalk, Ebble at, 132
Broadlands, Romsey—once Lord Palmerston's home, 102
Brocket, Lea at, 69
Brougham, Mr J. H.—a Wandle proprietor, 59
Brown Candover, Arle (Itchen) at, 108
Mr. J. H.—a Wandle proprietor, 59
Browne the Poet at Ottery, 149
on Tavy, 161
Brown Willy, Fowey near, 169
Broxbourne, Lea below, 70
Broxton Water, the, 157
Brushford, Barle at, 139
Brook, the, 140, 149
Buckland Brook, the, 162
"Lovers' Leap" at, 155
Bucklebury, Pang at, 95
Bude, the, 167
and Launceston Canal reservoir, 167
Bulbourne, the, 77
Bulford, Avon (Christchurch) at, 125
Bull inn at Fairford, 86
Bull Inn, Gerrard's Cross, 82
Buller, Colonel — his Char water, 121
Bullington, Test tributary at, 100
Bumbles, the, 14
Buntingford, Rib near, 72
Burford, Windrush at, 84

C

Cænis, 14
Calstock, Tamar at, 159
Camel, the, 168
Camelford, Camel near, 168
King's Arms hotel at, 168
Canterbury as angling headquarters, 49
Carey, the, 135
Carew, Sir Francis—at Beddington, 58
Cascade river, the, 167
Cassiobury Park, Gade at, 78
Catherston Leweston, Char at, 121
Carey, the, 159
Carlisle, Major—on Test Mayfly, 107
Castle Coombe, Box Brook at, 114
Cerne, the, 118
Chagford, Teign at, 153
Chalfont St. Giles, Misbourne at, 82
St. Peter, Misbourne, 82
Chalk stream flies, 10
streams in hot weather, 19
Char, the, 121
Chantrey at Houghton Club, 105
Chard, Isle at, 137
Junction, Axe at, 147
Charles II. at Denham Court, 64
Charlton, Anton at, 105
Avon (Christchurch) at, 125
Charmouth, Char at, 121
Clatworthy, Tone near, 137
Chelsea Bridge, 17
Chenies, Char at, 80
Cheriton, Itchen at, 108
Cherry Brook, the, 154, 155
Chesham, Chess at, 80
Chess, the, 32, 80
pollution of the, 18
Chew, the, 139
Magna, Chew at, 139
Stoke, Chew at, 139
Chewton Mendip, Chew at, 139
Chilbolton, Test at, 100, 103
Chilham Castle, 47
Chiltern Hills, 125

O

THE END

RICHARD CLAY AND SONS, LIMITED, LONDON AND BUNGAY.